RICH $AVAGE

Lock Down Publications and Ca$h
Presents
RICH $AVAGE
A Novel by *Martell "Troublesome" Bolden*

Rich $avage

Lock Down Publications
Po Box 944
Stockbridge, Ga 30281

Visit our website @
www.lockdownpublications.com

Lock Down Publications
Like our page on Facebook: Lock Down Publications @
www.facebook.com/lockdownpublications.ldp
Cover design and layout by: **Dynasty Cover Me**
Book interior design by: **Shawn Walker**
Edited by: **Kiera Northington**

Stay Connected with Us!

Text **LOCKDOWN** to 22828 to stay up-to-date with new
releases, sneak peaks, contests and more…
Thank you.

Submission Guideline.

Submit the first three chapters of your completed manuscript to ldpsubmissions@gmail.com, subject line: Your book's title. The manuscript must be in a .doc file and sent as an attachment. Document should be in Times New Roman, double spaced and in size 12 font. Also, provide your synopsis and full contact information. If sending multiple submissions, they must each be in a separate email.

Have a story but no way to send it electronically? You can still submit to LDP/Ca$h Presents. Send in the first three chapters, written or typed, of your completed manuscript to:

LDP: Submissions Dept
Po Box 944
Stockbridge, Ga 30281

DO NOT send original manuscript. Must be a duplicate.

Provide your synopsis and a cover letter containing your full contact information.

Thanks for considering LDP and Ca$h Presents.

Prologue

Countin' up cash, Ace stacked each bill in individual piles, while his nigga, Chedda, was rolling up a blunt. They were in the trap house seated on a worn out couch. On a good day, the trap brought in seven, eight G's. After moving all the work, they had shut down the trap for the night and first thing tomorrow, they would get in touch with the plug in order to re-up.

Chedda puffed the blunt a few times before handing it to Ace. He then stood and grabbed his .9mm, which lay beside Ace's .40 Glock atop the coffee table. They both made a habit of keeping their poles close, just in case.

"Hurry back so you can help me finish countin' up this cash," Ace told him.

"Won't nothin' keep me away from the cash for too long," Chedda said, wearing a grin as he headed for the bathroom.

Ace and Chedda were only up-and-comin' in the game. Ace held an average height with a trim build, had a low haircut with deep waves and brown skin. And at only nineteen, he had already seen a lot of shit. He had probably seen more than he shoulda seen when he was still on the porch. He'd seen some niggas get stripped, some niggas get indicted, some niggas get rich, and some niggas get murked. Then when he jumped off the porch, he'd seen all that shit up close and was prepared for what came with being in the trenches.

Chedda was his nigga since he and Ace had met a few years back in juvie, although he was a couple years older than Ace, they were tight. He was down to ride or die for Ace without a doubt, and had proven it many times before. Tall and slim, with long dreadlocks, light brown eyes which matched his skin complexion, and his torso sprayed with tatts, he was a pistol totin' paper chaser. Growing up mostly in foster homes, Chedda felt more at home in the streets.

Ace and Chedda's plan was to get their money and weight up in time. Thus far, between the both of them, they were only workin' with a quarter-brick of yae and about thirty G's. And they were down to trap or die in the streets.

After puffin' the blunt of loud once more, Ace placed it in the ashtray and went back to countin' up the paper-cheese. While he counted out a stack of twenties, suddenly the front door flew open. Two niggas pulled a kick-door on the trap house and bombarded inside, barefaced, brandishing guns.

"Your ass know what it is, nigga!" one of the niggas hissed as he ran up with his gun leveled on Ace, while the second nigga rushed over to the coffee table and began gathering up the money. Ace recognized one of the niggas from around the way, his name was Bullet.

Shit happened so sudden, Ace had no time to grab his .40 Glock. But lil did the niggas know, Chedda was in the bathroom strapped, and Ace was sure he had heard the commotion and would come out bustin'. In that moment it was either do or die, so Ace lunged forward, reaching for his gun.

Boc, boc!

Before Ace was able to reach his .40, Bullet popped him twice. The first slug hit him in the chest and the second landed in his stomach. Ace struggled to catch his breath while suffering terrible pain from the hot sensation of each slug. Once the cash was all gathered Bullet and his nigga ran out of the trap. Grabbing his pole, Ace managed to climb to his feet and then go after them niggas, wildly bustin' at 'em as he stumbled down the front porch steps. While continuing towards the car parked at the curb, the nigga Bullet returned shots. Each of their shots exploded in the stillness of the night and sparks lit up the darkness. Ace pulled the trigger until he emptied the thirty-shot stick. No longer having the strength to remain on his feet, Ace collapsed onto the sidewalk.

Right then Chedda came hurrying out of the trap and leaped off the porch, bustin' at the niggas. Once they hopped into the ride, Chedda filled it with bullet holes as it sped away down the street. Rushing over to Ace's aide, Chedda knelt and cupped his boy's head and pressed it against his chest. It was becoming difficult for Ace to breathe, and he began to cough up blood as he faded in and out of consciousness. Shit, in that moment, Ace didn't know whether he would live or die.

"Shit! Stay with me, my nigga. I got you. Fight that shit, Ace!" Chedda urged.

Ace tried staying with Chedda, but everything faded black...

Martell "Troublesome" Bolden

Chapter 1

Opening his eyes for the first time since blackin' out, Ace's vision was blurred. Also his throat was as dry as sandpaper and he was in hella pain. Being disoriented, he didn't realize where he was for a moment. Then he recalled that he'd been popped, so he had to be in the hospital with all of the machines he was hooked up to.

As his vision cleared, he noticed his sister, Mika, sitting at his bedside napping in the chair, and in a groggy voice Ace said, "Sis?"

"Hey, bro," Mika responded. "It's about time you're awake."

"How long's it been?" he managed to say, his voice groggy.

"Boy, your ass been laid up in this hospital for three days. Although the doctor says you're gonna be alright. They had to give you rush surgery in order to remove a bullet. Said it should take a few weeks for you to heal. At least you'll be able to be discharged from the hospital in a couple days."

Damn, this shit can't be real, Ace contemplated, although he knew that damn near losing his life was as real as it gets.

The surgery Ace had to have in order to have a bullet removed, which had been lodged in his chest, left him in hella pain and with about a nine-inch zipper down his stapled-up torso. With the condition he was in, maybe it was best for him to have to remain in the hospital for a day or two. But shit, he was ready to get back to the streets.

"Where's Glen? Why isn't lil bro here?" Ace asked. Glen was their fifteen-year-old baby brother.

"He wanted to be here but I needed him at home to watch Breon," Mika told him, referring to her son.

Chedda stepped into the room. "See your ass finally woke. You a'ight?" he said to Ace as he approached the bedside.

"I will be, once I murk the nigga who did this shit." Ace sat up in bed with the assistance of Chedda.

"Damn, Ace, thought I was gon' lose you," Chedda expressed.

Mika waved him off. "His ass alright. Look, I got to get back home. Just call if you need anything."

"Don't trip, Mika, I got him," Chedda told her.

"Alright then." Mika walked over to the counter and grabbed her purse and keys. "Call me." She gave Ace a ginger hug before heading out the room.

Once they were alone, Chedda's demeanor turned savage. "My nigga, did you get a look at who the fuck did this shit?" He was itchin' to know. More like his trigger finger was itchin'.

"Yeah, I did get a good look at the niggas, and I remember one of 'em from runnin' across him in the streets. It was the nigga Bullet. His bitch-ass is who popped me," Ace let him know.

"Soon as you get back to the streets then we gon' spin on that bitch-ass nigga ASAP," Chedda asserted. He peeped at his Rolly timepiece. "My nigga, I gotta get home to my bitch and shorty. You know how that shit goes. Just hit my line if you need anything." He and Ace shook up before Chedda bounced.

It was night out as Ace laid in bed. Staring at the TV uninterestedly, thoughts of nearly losin' his life churned in his head, and he doubted if Bullet even considered if he had managed to survive. Soon Bullet would get popped like Ace had gotten popped, but Bullet wouldn't be fuckin' breathin'.

...

The next morning, two detectives shook Ace outta a bad sleep looking to investigate the incident. The hospital was obligated to report all gunshot victims to the police. When Ace refused to cooperate with the investigation, the dicks began to treat him like he was being interrogated. And as usual, they played the good cop / bad cop roles. Each time Ace was asked something he told them he didn't see, didn't hear, or didn't know shit.

"You're a fuckin' liar!" bad cop, Detective Lucas, raved frustrated.

"Take it easy, Lucas," good cop, Detective Bradshaw, calmed his partner. He then turned to Ace and, for about the fifth time, asked, "Now really, who shot ya?"

"Like I told you before, I'ont know." Ace refused to snitch.

Detective Bradshaw stood from the chair. "If that's how you wanna play it, fine."

"I'm sure we'll be seeing you again around the neighborhood, whether it's dead or alive," Detective Lucas piped in.

Lucas and Bradshaw were two cops that didn't go by the book, they were rogue. Realizing they had no chance at getting Ace to snitch, the dicks decided to leave.

Ace wanted to get his justice in the streets.

Martell "Troublesome" Bolden

Chapter 2

After bein' discharged from the hospital a couple days later, Ace was ready to get back to the streets. Although he wasn't physically fit enough to do much due to the pain he was still in, wouldn't shit keep him from his motive to get rich in the streets.

While Chedda steered the white Nissan Maxima, Ace rode shotgun behind the tinted windows. "So, what's the word on the pussy-nigga Bullet? I'm ready hit his ass up," Ace said eagerly.

"So far, there's no word on his whereabouts. Don't trip, we'll find his ass," Chedda replied. He passed Ace the blunt of loud, and when Ace took a pull of the weed it caused him to cough and Chedda chuckled. "Nigga, just make sure you take shit slow in these streets."

"Fuck that. Ain't gon' let a couple slugs slow me down."

Chedda yielded the whip to a halt at the stoplight on 27th and North Street. "Ace, all I'm sayin' is you don't gotta rush into a war with the nigga Bullet. In the meantime, focus on gettin' money, 'cause a nigga can't go to war unless his money right," he stressed.

"I'ma focus on gettin' to the money. But, Chedda, whenever I find out where Bullet ass is, then it's all-out war," Ace swore.

"And you already know I'm down to go into war with you, my nigga." He smirked and held up the .9mm from his lap. And of course, Ace's .40 Glock laid across his own lap. After being popped up he didn't plan to be caught dead without it.

Ace's iPhone buzzed, and once he checked its display a smile crept across his lips when he noticed the call was from a shorty he'd recently met and was feelin'. Her name was Paris. He answered, "What's good, lil baby?"

"Ace, why have your ass been ghostin' me lately?" Paris said heatedly.

"It ain't even like that. I just was in the hospital for a few days, that's all." Ace hit the blunt and then passed it to Chedda as he pulled off at the greenlight.

"My bad. Are you okay? What happened?" she asked, sounding concerned.

"Yeah, I'm a'ight. Just a nigga caught me slippin' and he popped me."

"Oh, my God! I'm glad you're alright, Ace. If there's anything I can do to help then just lemme know," she offered.

"I'll keep that in mind," he assured her. After telling Paris he'd call her whenever he was free, they ended the call.

It was afternoon when Ace and Chedda arrived in the hood. With it being summer, the hood was lively. Niggas were hanging on the corners servin' fiends, bitches flaunted their assets, lil hood children cluttered the streets and sidewalks playing games, while the elders watched it all from their porches. There was no place like being in the hood.

Ace peeped Mika standing near a silver Jaguar, talking with one of the many niggas that tried getting with her. He was used to niggas sweatin' her on the regular. *I bet he's a fuck-boy like the rest,* Ace thought. Only nigga Mika had been with that Ace respected was her baby's daddy, Tim, because before being murked he was savage with his. And Ace knew part of Mika was trying to fill that void.

Curvaceously plus-size, with sandy brown skin and naturally long hair, Mika was a very attractive girl at twenty-four. And being independent with her own car, house, and a job, she didn't need a nigga for a damn thing. But like most single ladies, she seemed to always find herself in toxic relationships with the hopes that it'll get better.

Seeing Reverend Johnson sitting out on his porch, Ace knew Rev would have a preach and prayer for him, which Ace wasn't even tryna hear. Reverend Johnson had been a very close friend to Ace's granny for many years before she passed from cancer. So Rev felt a need to save Ace from an early grave. But the only thing that could save Ace was his pistol and his slugs.

"Go around back through the alley," Ace urged Chedda, who bust out laughing, knowing that Ace was tryna duck Reverend Johnson.

"My nigga, you can't duck Rev forever," Chedda told him.

"Nigga, just pull up in the alley."

Chedda braked the Maxima to a stop in the alley behind the crib Ace lived with his sister and younger brother. When their Granny passed away she had left the home to their moms, but their moms was upstate doing fed time for the past three years behind charges of drug trafficking. As for their pops, he had been an avid jack boy who got smoked during a lick. So Ace and Mika and Glen was left to fend for themselves.

"I'ma hit up the plug while waitin' on you," Chedda said as Ace stepped out the whip.

"Make sure you let him know to meet us at the spot."

After Ace went and retrieved his half of the re-up money and returned to the whip, he and Chedda headed around the corner to the trap spot they held down. They'd paid a fiend to let them trap outta her house. While sitting on the front porch steps waiting on the plug, Ace noticed three niggas a couple places down posted in front of their own trap. They were packboys for an opp of Ace's named Stone.

"I ain't about to let the nigga Stone think he takin' shit over," Ace stated.

"Stone got his niggas pushin' work and airin' shit out all around the hood like he tryna take over," Chedda added.

Ace stood from the porch and pulled his pole from his waist. "Let's show the nigga Stone who this hood belongs to."

"Say no more." Chedda drew his own pole.

Stepping down the block, Ace and Chedda approached the packboys, who immediately peeped their guns in hand. One of the packboys, a chubby light skinned nigga named Duke, looked as though he was tempted to go for his own gun, until Ace held them all at gunpoint. Then Duke stood down, not wanting to catch a slug. So that none of the packboys could make any moves, Chedda frisked them all and confiscated the pistol from the nigga Duke's waist. Ace and Chedda wanted the packboys to let Stone know they weren't going for a hostile takeover.

"You niggas send Stone a message that we ain't havin' him takin' shit over around here. And if we have to do it ourselves, then we'll send him that message by leavin' one of you bodied," Ace warned them.

"Now move the fuck around," Chedda ordered.

Once the packboys cleared the block, Ace and Chedda made their way back to their trap house. Shortly thereafter, a red Range Rover pulled to a stop in front of the trap, it belonged to the plug, Baller. The two made their way towards the Range and entered the rear seat, being that Baller's right-hand man, Phat, rode shotgun. Baller pulled off, taking a spin around the block.

Since Ace and Chedda started trappin' as young teens, Baller had been their plug. Actually they had run off on the plug with the first pack he'd ever fronted them, and instead of Baller making an example out of them, he decided to make them work off the debt of the pack and give them the game. Mainly because Baller recognized the two young savages had what it takes to get rich. Baller was a light-skinned, slim nigga with long braids and gold teeth. He was about his money and wouldn't hesitate to send his shooters if a nigga needed to pay in blood.

"Same yae, same price," Baller said as he bent the corner. He glanced over to Phat and nodded, then Phat pulled out a quarter-bird and passed it back to Ace, and in exchange Chedda gave him the re-up money. Before stuffing the cash inside the Burberry tote bag with the rest, Phat quickly counted up the cash and made sure it was all there.

Glancing at Ace through the rearview mirror, Baller said, "Heard what happened to you. For a nigga who just got popped, you out here in these trenches like it ain't shit."

"I been out here and I'ma be out here. Ain't shit change," Ace replied evenly.

After spinning around the block, Baller pulled to the curb in front of the trap. Chedda hopped out the Range and as Ace began to follow suit, Baller halted him. "Check it out, Ace. Either bein' in these trenches gon' make you get rich, or make you into a savage. Just don't let it make you a murder victim."

"Baller, you don't have to worry about me. I'm made for these trenches," Ace told him. The two shook up and then Ace stepped out the Range.

As Baller headed down the street, Ace and Chedda headed into the trap house to cook up the yae.

•••

Due to Ace's full-time trap weeks came and went after his discharge from the hospital. Although he was still in some pain from the surgery, he didn't let that stop him nor slow him down from trappin'. And normally Ace was in trap mode with Chedda, whenever Chedda's baby's mama didn't have a leash on his ass. Ace and Chedda were trying to get their money and weight up, even if that meant them having to make the streets bleed murder.

Ace parked the Maxima outside the corner store located in the hood. While he went inside Chedda chilled in the whip. Inside the store Ace greeted the Arab, Abdul, who stood behind the counter at the cash register. They were familiar with one another due to seeing each other frequently there. Abdul and his family were from the Middle East, but he tried hard to fit in with the Western culture by even going as far as dressing urban. Ace took a liking to him.

"A box of Swisher Sweets blunts and a lighter," Ace requested and handed over a twenty.

"If you ever want some reefer that's better than you've ever had, then I'm your man." Abdul smirked. His Middle Eastern accent was noticeable. He slid the items and change to Ace and added, "In fact, if you need anything just ask."

"I'll keep that in mind." Ace was sure Abdul meant what he'd said.

After purchasing the items Ace headed out the store. Outside, he peeped an opp of his, Stone, posted up with a few of his boys. Ace dug into his hoodie and gripped his Glock, ready to pop off.

Stone was a nigga from Chicago who had relocated to Milwaukee a couple years back and brought along a few of his boys. Over time he had managed to form himself a gang and gained a rep for gettin' money and leaving bodies in his wake. His problem with Ace stemmed from Ace refusing to join his gang and standing in the way of Stone taking over the hood. Stone was dark-skinned, bulky, with a bald fade and gold teeth. Although he was a trap nigga, Stone wouldn't hesitate to put in gun work.

On sight Stone and his boys closed in on Ace. Peeping what was going down, Chedda cocked the slide of his steel before slipping out of the Maxima and he coolly leaned back up against the whip, holding his .9 concealed in hand, ready to bust.

"Say, shorty, what's this shit about you comin' at some of my boys?" Stone wanted to know with hostility in his tone.

"Stone, you and your boys best move around, or else," Ace asserted.

Stone nudged the nigga Duke who stood at his side and scoffed, "Nigga think he's bulletproof all of a sudden. Just stay the fuck away from my boys, Ace. Unless you want some smoke."

"And I'm sure I'll be the nigga still standing when the smoke clears." Ace shouldered Stone on his way towards the whip. He noticed Chedda keeping a close eye on Stone and his boys all the way up until he and Chedda stepped into the whip and dipped off.

While Chedda was rolling up a blunt, he said, "That nigga Stone gon' become a problem sooner or later. He's not gonna let us keep pressin' his boys and losin' him money without eventually beefin' with us. And we can't afford beef until our money right."

"So we gotta make sure we gettin' more money than Stone and the rest of these niggas in the streets. Because if they want beef, then I'ma give it to 'em," Ace replied brashly. He steered towards the block.

"Then we'll cop more weight on our next re-up and flood the hood. But first we need to flip the work we already have." Chedda set flames to the blunt and puffed it a few times before passing it to his boy.

"That's our next move."

Ace pulled the Maxima to the curb at his crib. He and Chedda stepped out the whip and posted on the block. The two served crack-heads as they came and went by the drove, all while entertaining a few bitches from around the hood. Of them all, a bitch named Star was on Ace's dick, and she was one of the baddest bitches the hood had to offer.

Star always had niggas sweatin' her on the regular, being only nineteen with a caramel tone, slim-thick shape, and a very pretty face. Her hair and nails stayed done courtesy of niggas cashin' her out. She liked the attention from niggas but wanted it most from Ace. Maybe it was because he had been the first nigga who fucked her. But she tried acting all stuck up, like she didn't need Ace, or no nigga.

Ace was seated on his porch steps while on the phone talking with Paris when Star came walking by, headed towards Neesha's crib. He thought she was looking like a snack in her form fitting Nike tracksuit. Ending the call, Ace stopped Star. "You just gonna walk by a nigga like you don't see me sittin' here," he said.

"Ace, it's not even like that," Star replied coolly. She couldn't seem to resist his bad boy image.

"You can stop actin' all stuck up and shit with me, Star. We both know you want me." Ace smirked.

Star smacked her sexy lips. "Nigga, if I want you then I can have you... any time, any place."

"Is that right?"

"You haven't left."

Ace stood from the steps and moved near her. "Then what you waitin' on?"

"You."

Slipping his arm around her slim waist, Ace led Star inside his crib and to his bedroom. He wasted no time planting kisses on her lips and neck as he palmed her ass in both hands. She enjoyed the feel of him all over her. Dropping onto her knees, Star removed the gun from his waist and set it on the nightstand before undoing Ace's RockStar jeans, letting them fall down around his AirMax sneakers, and then pulled out his stiff dick and slid it into her warm mouth. She twirled her tongue around its tip and down to the sac while pumping its shaft in her petite hand.

"Damn boo, you suckin' this dick so right," Ace groaned. Palming the back of her head, he fucked Star's pretty face as she deep-throated his piece. The warmth and wetness of her mouth on his hardness drove him wild! Star sucked and slurped on the pipe until Ace shot semen down her throat, and she tasted every drop.

Ace then pulled Star's bottoms down around her knees and bent her over the bed, he slipped on a rubber before digging his hardness deep inside her wet-shot from behind. He pounded her pussy while gripping her ass and she arched her back.

Looking back at it over her shoulder, Star moaned, "Yes, Ace! Just like that, baby!"

Star's pussy was as good as the first time Ace had ever fucked her. But she wasn't his girl, so no matter how good the pussy was he never claimed it as his own. He didn't know how Star may have felt but for him it was about a quick fuck as usual, no feelings involved.

As Ace began digging her out deeper and harder from behind, Star buried her face into the bed and let out muffled screams of pleasure. His stiff dick felt so damn amazing inside her slippery pussy. As he hit her spot Star's wetness began to cum like a water flow. Some strokes later, Ace busted a nut.

Following the quickie, Ace pulled up his jeans and returned his pole on his waist. He told her, "Don't think this make you my bitch, Star. It's just a quick fuck."

"Ace, I ain't one of those bitches who be on your dick. It was just a quick fuck for me too," Star replied with an attitude as she pulled up her bottoms.

"Bitches like you come a dime a dozen."

"And niggas like you ain't shit!"

Back out on the block, Ace n'em were seated on Neesha's porch smoking a blunt. Neesha's crib was where most of the bitches from around the way hung out. Neesha was a ghetto-ass, gossiping type. She was brown-skinned, average in looks, and a heavier girl after having three kids at only twenty-two. Though she was a drama queen, Neesha was good people.

While on the phone with one of her homegirls, Neesha was talking all loud. "You mean the light-skinned nigga with dreads. His name's Bullet. He be over on 29th and Hampton Street. Ugh, girl, I don't see how you like Bullet's ugly ass," she was saying.

This caught Ace's attention. All of Neesha's damn gossiping was useful, little did she know. But Ace knew better than to mention anything to her about it. He stepped off the porch and headed over to Chedda where he stood on the corner with some niggas from the hood.

"I know where to find the nigga Bullet," Ace told Chedda.

"And how you find this out?" Chedda asked.

"Neesha happened to be runnin' her lips about the nigga. She mentioned what hood he be in. I'm talkin' about ridin' out tonight." Chedda noticed murder in Ace's eyes.

"Then let's ride or die."

Rich $avage

•••

Silence filled the sedan as Ace and Chedda, along with two other niggas from their hood, West and Creep, rode under the dark sky. West was the designated driver, Creep rode shotgun, and Ace and Chedda took up the backseat. The whole car was strapped, and that's not talking seatbelts. West circled the block as they all surveyed the area for Bullet. He then parked near the corner where they had a clear view of the street.

"There the nigga is now." Chedda spotted Bullet and pointed him out as he and two other niggas exited the blue Impala that had just pulled to the curb and parked.

Ace immediately recognized Bullet and was eagerly ready to air him out. He implored, "Spin on that pussy-ass nigga!"

The headlights were out as the sedan crept down the block towards Bullet and his niggas. Everyone in the sedan made sure their heaters were ready for action. Once they pulled up on Bullet unsuspected, Ace hung out the window, letting his Draco ride sideways.

Boc, boc, boc, boc, boc, boc!

Bullet instantly got low beside the Impala once the shots rang out. He then drew his own weapon and his niggas followed suit, they began bustin' back. A swarm of bullets violently struck the sedan and caused Ace to duck inside out of harm's way. With a blast from the Mossberg pump, Creep blew one of Bullet's niggas backwards into the side of the Impala, leaving him slumped. Chedda spit fire from his .9mm at Bullet's remaining nigga, dropping him with four shots to the chest. Ace opened up the Draco and Swiss-cheesed the side of the Impala, flattening tires and shattering windows in his attempt to hit up Bullet. All the while, Bullet

25

didn't let up on returning fire. Suddenly a slug pushed Creep's shit back, causing blood and brain matter to splatter about the interior of the sedan and some onto West.

Bullet began to retreat and immediately Ace hopped outta the sedan and chased after him, lettin' off the Draco. Without looking back, Bullet fired shots over his shoulder towards Ace in order to prevent Ace from getting a clear shot at him. Hastily Bullet then fled through a gangway between two apartment buildings, and once Ace went to air out the gangway behind him, he was caught off guard as Bullet was standing there awaiting him with his pole aimed and ready.

Blocka, blocka, blocka!

Slugs narrowly zipped by Ace causing him to duck out the way, which gave Bullet the opportunity to slip away. Once Ace hurried back to the sedan, West sped away from the murder scene. Several blocks away, West turned into an alley where he pulled the sedan into a vacant garage behind an abandoned house. They each thoroughly wiped clean the inside and outside of the sedan of any fingerprints before they fled on foot. It fucked each of them up to have to leave Creep for dead, but there was nothing they could do to save him.

Ace was heated as hell that the pussy-ass nigga Bullet happened to slip away. It had been damn near three months since Bullet popped him up, and if he wasn't aware that Ace had lived then, Bullet should understand that dead men can't retaliate.

Chapter 3

Since the shootout, Ace stayed in trap mode over the past couple weeks. He was sure Bullet would eventually retaliate and he would be prepared to ride or die. Until then, Ace knew it was money to be made in the streets.

He and Chedda began moving the weight they had gotten from Baller, they had copped a half key and Baller fronted them the second half. They already had several trap niggas throughout the hood they served weight to. Also they rocked up half of the work in order to make a greater profit off the kilo. Ace and Chedda were establishing themselves as trap gods in the streets.

Ace pulled the Maxima to the curb. He was about to catch a play from a neighborhood smoker, Sly. As Sly approached the whip, Ace dashed down the passenger window.

"S'up, Sly?" Ace asked.

"You know me, tryna make a couple bucks. Speakin' of," Sly leaned into the window. "So I got this broad in my place who's lookin' to spend some good money."

"Hop in so we can talk." Ace popped the door lock and Sly hopped inside the whip. "So, what's the deal?"

"Like I was sayin', I got this broad who just cashed her check and she wants to buy an eight ball. I'm sure she'll want more after she gets high. All you gotta do is provide me with the work, and then me and you both can get paid," Sly explained.

Ace pulled out his sack and handed Sly the eight ball, and then Sly stepped out the car and made his way inside the run-down apartment complex where he resided. Ace knew Sly meant he would overcharge the broad for the eighth of crack. Baldhead and skinny, Sly kept himself up to par for a smoker. Ace had been knowing Sly ever since he could remember, and he had heard that back before Sly has gotten turned out on crack, he used to be a drug boss. Even still, Sly hustled on the side when he wasn't gettin' high on his own supply.

A moment later Sly returned to the car and handed Ace his profits. "There's your proper chop. Be expectin' a call from me later for some more work."

"Just don't call me for nothin' less than an eight-ball," Ace instructed him before pulling off. He knew that once he got his weight up, having someone like Sly on the payroll would be beneficial.

Ace steered towards the trap and puffed on a blunt as he listened to Lil Baby's "Cash." He spotted the unmarked Dodge Magnum, which was occupied by two narcs, Detectives Lucas and Bradshaw. The two narcs were well known around the hood for being dirty cops. The Magnum was nearly halfway down the block as Ace cruised towards it, he put the blunt in the ashtray and turned down the music. He was riding dirty with his sack and stick so he didn't want to give the narcs any probable cause to pull him over, then again he knew they didn't need any.

As the Magnum passed by, Ace knew the narcs had their mugs fixated on his car being that they had it out for him. Through the rearview mirror Ace peeped the Magnum hastily committing a U-turn. Knowing the narcs were after him, Ace sped down the street and at the corner he made a sharp turn, and then at the next corner he made another in his attempt to shake the narcs. Turning onto a side street, Ace offed the headlights and whipped the Maxima to the curb betwixt two parked vehicles. Being that it was night outside, it wouldn't be so easy for the narcs to spot the whip, but to play it safe Ace sat parked for a moment and continued smoking the blunt, not wanting to make a move just yet. Sure the narcs were scouting the area kept him at a standstill, Ace knew he had to be vigilant if he didn't want the dirty cops, Lucas and Bradshaw catching him riding dirty. He'd rather hold court in the streets.

Shortly thereafter, Ace decided to dip to the block. He parked outside of his crib and then stepped out the whip and made his way over to Chedda, who was posted up with some of the hood niggas.

"You look shook. What is it?" Chedda wanted to know. He took a drag of his cigarette.

"Just had to flee from the dirty-ass cops Lucas and Bradshaw. I ain't with lettin' Twelve or no nigga shake me down," Ace told him.

Chedda exhaled smoke. "That's why we gotta be on our toes in these streets, Ace, 'cause they waitin' to catch us slippin' out here. Now that we're gettin' our weight and money up, we need to keep a low profile."

"I hear you, Chedda. That don't mean I won't blow a nigga down in these streets if need be. Just means I'ma put the money first."

"I'm with you on that."

After postin' on the block for a while, Ace got a call from Sly about coppin' more work. As he and Chedda headed for the whip, they were stopped by Reverend Johnson, who was standing on his porch. Ace still hadn't taken time to talk with Rev, he just really didn't care to hear Rev preach at him. Rev waved over both Ace and Chedda and invited them into his modest home. He sat across from Ace and Chedda in the living room, studying them with humbling eyes.

"So son, how are you doing?" Rev asked Ace.

"Much better now," Ace replied. He was mostly recovered from his wounds.

"Good, thank God. You're blessed to be alive." Rev leaned back in his seat. "Let me ask you two fine young brothers a very thoughtful question, what is it to gain the world only to lose your soul? You see, the devil will tempt you with everything this world has to offer, good and bad, but all you two need in this world is to follow God's plan." He preached with reason.

Rev always tryna change a nigga life with this God shit, Ace contemplated annoyed.

Nearly an hour dragged by before Reverend Johnson ended his sermon. Once Ace and Chedda were back outside, Chedda was heated as hell at Ace for getting him caught up in Rev's preach.

"Damn nigga, if it wasn't for your ass then I wouldna had to listen to Rev's long, borin'-ass preach and shit." Chedda scoffed as they were headed to Ace's whip.

Ace chuckled. "My nigga, you probably needed to hear it more than me."

"Yeah right. All due respect, Rev can miss me with that God is good, God is great shit."

"Ace?" Reverend Johnson called after Ace from his porch. He had one final question as an afterthought.

"Yessir?" Ace stopped in his tracks.

"Does it matter if you live to be old or die young?"

Ace pondered a moment. "Not really."

•••

Paris opened the front door to find Ace standing there. "Hey," she greeted him.

Rich $avage

"S'up, boo." Ace played it cool. Paris wrapped her arms around his neck and he reached around and palmed her ass.

"Ace, would you stop! You so damn mannish!" she giggled and playfully pushed him away.

"Damn, Paris, you lookin' good with all that ass on you." Ace smirked. He admired how good she looked with minimal makeup on. Paris was every bit of gorgeous. Her long pixie cut brought of her facial features. Her cheek bones were high and sculpted, and her sandy brown eyes were doll-like. She stood five-four and weighed a hundred and fifteen pounds, with a petite but curvy body. Only twenty-one years old, shorty had a nice apartment, a car, and worked at a daycare. Paris was definitely on her shit.

Ace had dropped by Paris's apartment to scoop her up and take her out on date. "You ready to ride?" he asked.

"Yeah. Just lemme grab my bag," Paris told him. She stepped inside for a moment before returning with her Versace handbag and then locking up her place. As they approached the Maxima, Paris said, "What're you doing?"

Ace stepped to the passenger side and pulled open the door. "You'll be drivin'."

"And why's that?" she wanted to know.

"'Cause I'm riding with my gun on me, and since you have L's it'll be better that you drive, just in case we get pulled over by Twelve," he explained and then stepped inside the car and she followed.

Paris looked to him and naively asked, "And how come you carry a gun?"

"Rather be caught with it than without it in these streets," he simply told her.

Paris just shook her head and started the car then pulled off.

On the way to their destination they smoked on a blunt and made small talk. Moneybagg Yo's "Match My Fly" played at a lowered volume in the background.

"You're the first nigga I been out with in a while," Paris admitted.

"And I don't take out many girls," Ace responded.

"How come you don't?" She pulled to a halt at a red light.

"I just normally prefer to keep things casual."

Paris furrowed her arched brows and replied, "You mean like casual sex?"

Ace chuckled. "Sex don't have nothin' to do with it. Unless that's what you want." He puffed the blunt.

"Boy, whatevs!" Paris smiled.

They arrived at the movie theater. During the movie Ace and Paris shared a bucket of popcorn, they fed each other some and tossed a few puffs at one another. They laughed their asses off at Tiffany Haddish's comical acting in the film. For most of the movie, Paris couldn't keep her hands to herself. The more Ace was with her the more he was feelin' her.

Following the movie, they made their way to grab a bite to eat and some drinks at the well-known local spot Michael's. Ace ordered steak and potatoes and ordered Paris the same dish. They both had a glass of Hennessy.

"I usually don't date street niggas but there's some good about you that I like," Paris commented, finding his street edge sexy. She sipped at her drink.

"Yeah, well, street niggas can be good in our own ways. And it's always best to have someone to bring the good out," Ace replied.

"Do you treat all of your girls so nice?"

"So, you're my girl now?" He smirked.

Paris shifted in her seat and crossed her legs. "That's not what I meant."

"And why don't you have a nigga in your life?"

"Because I don't need a nigga to take care of me."

"And I respect that, but having a nigga won't make you less independent."

"You really have a different way about yourself, and I haven't met many niggas like you before," she conceded.

"That's 'cause I ain't just another nigga like them other niggas you've met," he told her.

The two enjoyed their meals over conversation. There was a vibe between them, even though they were different in ways. After leaving the restaurant they returned to Paris's apartment. Their date went so well, Paris suggested Ace stay the night with her and he obliged.

While Ace sat on the loveseat in the bedroom awaiting Paris, who was taking a shower, he rolled up a blunt. His iPhone buzzed, indicating he received a text. Checking its display, he noticed the text was from Star. He read it.

STAR:
Come thru and chill.

She can forget about it, Ace thought and sparked the blunt. Knowing he could get with Star anytime he preferred to spend the night with Paris. He replied via text.

ACE:
Maybe next time.

STAR:
Lemme guess, you with some bitch?

ACE:
And? You ain't my bitch. Like I said, maybe next time.

STAR:

Whateva Ace!

It wasn't long before Paris walked into the bedroom. She was ass naked and stood right in front of Ace. He leered at her from head to toe. Her titties were perky and her ass was plump. She had a piercing on her navel. And her mani/pedi was fresh and matching. Paris was so sexy that Ace's dick grew hard in his jeans. She knelt before him and as she undid his jeans, he held the blunt out for her and she took a pull of the loud. Pulling out his hard, long dick, Paris sucked the tip while jacking its shaft in her hand. She looked up at Ace and he watched her face him while he continued smoking the blunt. He relaxed back against the seat and allowed Paris to please his hardness with her soft lips.

"Shit baby, you got a nigga dick so ready," Ace grunted as Paris deep-throated him. He palmed the back of her head and began guiding her mouth rapidly up and down on his dick. Feeling a nut swell up in its tip, he pulled her head back, not wanting to bust just yet. "Climb on top of me," he instructed and Paris straddled his lap and he palmed her ass cheeks in both hands as she slid her wet pussy down on his pole.

"Yaass, Ace! It's so damn good!" Paris moaned in pleasure while Ace slammed her up and down on his dick. He sucked and nibbled on her erect nipples and she tossed her head back, enjoying how damn good he made her feel. "Lemme ride this big-ass dick," she told him. Getting into the squat position, Paris slid down on the dick all the way to its base and up to its tip, taking in every inch of Ace. "Oh, my goodness, Ace, I'm cumming!" she exclaimed as she came like a waterfall. Her pussy was so snug and slippery and warm wrapped around Ace's hardness.

Ace loved the feeling of her twat engulfing his whole erection. "Damn, Paris, this pussy the truth!" he breathed. No longer able to hold it back, Ace busted a nut deep inside Paris's wetness and nutted stronger than he'd ever nutted. He pulled her mouth onto his and kissed her hungrily, their tongues making love. Ace stood while holding Paris and walked her over to the bed where he laid her back. He then knelt in between her legs and began to feast on the pussy.

"Ooh, yesss... Eat it, Ace, eat it just like that," Paris groaned. She palmed his head while he flicked his tongue over her clit. Her pussy became juicy and Ace slurped and lapped up her juices, causing shorty to arch her back off the bed and push his mouth onto her pussy. He feasted on her good-good until her body began to rack with orgasms. "Mmm, yes, Ace! Yes!"

After fuckin' and suckin', they both climbed into bed and fell fast asleep. Paris was the epitome of a lady in the streets and a freak in the bed. And Ace enjoyed her being his lil freak. The two didn't have much in common, with her being a good girl and him a street nigga, however they were very attracted to each other. And tonight made them realize just how much they wanted to be together.

When Ace awoke the next morning, Paris was lying beside him with her head rested on his chest, while gingerly running her fingertips over the scar on his torso. He combed through her shorter hair with his fingers and kissed her forehead. *Shorty a nice sight for a nigga to wake up to*, Ace thought introspectively.

"Mornin'," he said to her.

"Good morning to you too." Paris smiled. "Would you like for me to cook some breakfast for you?"

"Smart, sexy, and can cook. Now that's wifey material!" Ace replied smoothly.

"Then put a ring on it," Paris responded as she slid out of bed. "Look, I set out some things for you in the bathroom."

She headed out the room and into the kitchen. Paris had already taken a shower and all and dressed herself in pajamas.

Once Ace took care of his nine and dressed himself, he made his way into the kitchen and sat at the small table. Paris made him a plate of scrambled eggs, bacon, and pancakes. Her cooking was better than he had expected. Ace knew Paris was the right type of bitch for him, and he wanted to keep her close.

"So, you never exactly told me why you're single," Ace said. He took a bite of bacon.

Paris shifted in her seat. "Well, the last nigga I was with turned out to be too controlling and could be very jealous. And at times it made him abusive towards me. I did everything for him, even things that went against my morals, and he still didn't seem to appreciate having me. So I decided to leave his ass," she expounded.

"Just know that you won't have to worry about no shit like that with me. I'll treat you better than that," Ace told her.

After breakfast, Ace had to get going. Paris showed him out to the car where they hugged and kissed. "Be careful in them streets, Ace," she advised him out of concern.

"I rather be caught with it than without it, remember." Ace smirked and patted the pole on his waist as he stepped into the whip. He pulled off, going on his way to handle his street affairs.

Chapter 4

Over the past few months, Ace and Chedda increasingly got their money and weight up. They had stacked over fifty G's and was playing with a brick. By then they could hardly ever be found on the block servin' smokers, instead they had packboys, while Ace and Chedda served weight. And Ace had recruited Sly to run his and Chedda's trap houses, and Sly turned out to be beneficial. Although Ace and Chedda still didn't have the streets on lock, their names were buzzing throughout the streets.

Ace pulled up in front of the crib. He stepped out the Maxima and made his way inside. As of late, he'd barely been there, being that he was now living with Paris. But he still stashed money and work there. Upon entering, Ace found Mika seated on the couch in the front room, she was smoking a cigarette while on the phone. He went into his old bedroom that Glen made his own, and Ace grabbed the four ounces of yae he'd stashed in the wall. On his way out Mika stopped him.

"Ace, I spoke with Mama. She says she misses you," Mika told him.

"And why should I give a fuck when she ain't never did shit for us, Mika," Ace replied bitterly.

"Don't be that way."

"If it wasn't for Grandma takin' us in then we woulda ended up in the system. So the only person I miss is Grandma." Ace didn't know his mother much because she was too damn busy in the streets to raise him or his siblings. Mika knew how he felt and always tried convincing him to forgive their mom.

"Bro, she's a changed woman now. Maybe you need to talk with her for yourself."

"Listen sis, next time Mama calls, tell her don't even ask about me," Ace told her. He changed the topic. "Anyway, who's that new nigga I been seein' you with lately?"

"His name's Keith. He's a good nigga."

"Bet he ain't shit like Tim." Ace scoffed.

Mika couldn't look him in the eyes. "Ace, what I had with Tim, I won't share with no nigga. But I really like Keith."

"As long as the nigga treat you right then I'll respect what you have with him," he assured. "Look, I gotta go and catch a play."

Outside, it was the fall season with winter fast approaching. Most hustlers used the winter season to grind and stack their paper up so they could pull out when the summer time hit. No matter the season, money, murder, and mayhem was abundant in the trenches.

As Ace walked down the porch steps he noticed Reverend Johnson raking up the fall leaves on his lawn and shot him a head nod, and Rev returned a wave of the hand. Whenever Rev wasn't at church he kept a watchful eye on the neighborhood.

Ace made his way to Neesha's place. She was seated on her porch with Star, they were smoking a blunt.

"Hey, Ace," Neesha greeted him. "You wanna hit this blunt?"

Ace grabbed the blunt and took a pull. "Have you seen Glen?"

"Not lately. But I'll let you know if I do," she replied.

"Do that." Ace passed the blunt to Star. He knew she felt some type of way that he'd been ghosting her ass lately.

"Ace, why you be actin' like you don't know my girl Star feelin' you and shit?"

Star nudged her. "Girl, would you leave me out of it. Ace doin' him, like I'm doin' me," she commented.

"You know I can fuck you if I want you, Star," Ace said, sure of himself.

"Whateva!" Star couldn't resist Ace even if she wanted to.

Ace headed to his whip and went on his way. He was to meet up with Chedda at the trap spot where they would cook up the yae. They had a couple niggas looking to cop some work from them.

On his way to the spot, Ace peeped a huddle of gamblers shooting dice in an alley. He pulled over the Maxima and decided to join in. Approaching the huddle he recognized a few of the gamblers from around the hood. Nine, who was handling the dice, was the only one he'd known personally. Looking to get a side bet on Nine, Ace placed a twenty on the pavement.

"Bet he hit his point," Ace offered to no one in particular.

"Bet." The fat nigga covered Ace's wager.

Nine shook up the dice and then rolled them over the pavement. Eventually he rolled craps, losing Ace his money. After several of the gamblers had their turn on the dice, it was Ace's turn. Once again Fatso and some others faded Ace's wagers on the dice. Out the gate, Ace rolled a seven and collected his winnings. By the time he'd gotten a turn to shoot the dice a few rounds, he lost nearly three racks in the gamble.

"Yo Ace, you leavin' already? You don't want a chance to get your money back?" Nine said as Ace headed for his car.

"Gambling don't come with a money back guarantee," Ace responded. *But I'ma be back for my money for sure*, he contemplated with malice aforethought.

Ace jumped in his whip and then drove around the corner, where he parked out of sight. He then grabbed his pole and tossed his hood over his head before hopping out the car. Making his way through a gangway with his gun in hand, Ace came upon the huddle of gamblers who were oblivious to his approach.

"Nobody move, nobody get murked," Ace growled as he hurried out the gangway with his gun leveled on the gamblers. "Now lay it the fuck down."

"It's like that, Ace?" Nine cried out as he and the others lay on the pavement.

"Nigga, it's straight like that."

Ace stripped the whole gamble taking everyone's monies. Afterwards he slipped through the gangway and hurried back to his whip. As he sped off he knew strippin' Nine and the others could come with beef, but Ace wasn't duckin' beef with no nigga.

Pulling up before the trap spot, Ace parked. He stepped out the car and then made his way inside and found Sly in the front room tending to the spot. Sly made sure all of the spots stayed with supply in order to serve the clientele and he always tested the product before it was distributed to the spots to make sure it was some of the best work in the hood. Ace and Chedda liked having him around because Sly was another set of eyes to look out for them. "S'up, Sly? I see you been doin' good, holdin' down the spots and shit," Ace said.

"I was a hustla before so I know what I'm doin'," Sly replied.

"Keep up the good work and get yourself clean, then maybe we'll put you on. Where's Chedda?"

"In the kitchen playin' chef."

Upon entering the kitchen, Ace found Chedda standing over the stove whipping up crack in a Pyrex. Their whip-game was proper, having learned from Baller as lil niggas, they could stretch the yae with the correct measurements of baking soda and still bring back straight-drop crack cocaine. The stench of cooked crack wafted in the air as Chedda was scraping the crack residue from the Pyrex with a wire hanger. "Fuck took you so long to be right back? You know we got niggas waitin' on us for this cook-up."

"On my way I got caught up in a gamble and shit. My bad," Ace told him. He set-out his four ounces of coke on the counter.

"How much money you lose this time around in the gamble?" Chedda was aware that his nigga was an avid gambler and that he would lose all of his money trying to win it all back.

"Nothin' 'cause I made the whole gamble run me my money back and some." Ace smirked.

"You with that gamblin' shit." Chedda shook his damn head. He set aside the crack he had cooked up to let it dry and harden. "Anyway. Niggas supposed to be here in about an hour for the work. So get that shit cooked up."

After the crack was cooked, Ace and Chedda let Sly give it a test. He stuffed his crack pipe with a crack rock and sucked on the glass dick. Sly's eyes bulged as he felt the elation of the drug. He confirmed the shit was straight-drop.

Shortly thereafter, there was a knock at the front door and as precaution, Ace and Chedda grabbed their guns. Peeping out from behind the window blind, Chedda seen it was the niggas they were to serve the weight. He let them in while Ace stood with his pole in hand, just in case. Since Ace was on security, Chedda made the transaction and served the niggas a nine-piece and one of the niggas named

Show weighed up the product on a digital scale to make sure the two hundred and fifty-two grams was all there, then in turn he paid up eight G's which Chedda counted out. It was just the way the game went.

"Just so y'all know, the nigga Stone tried offerin' to plug me on the yae tip. And when I told him I'm fuckin' with y'all, he got to talkin' cash shit about how y'all won't be in the game for long if it's up to him," Show informed.

"That nigga work isn't as good as our shit," Chedda said.

"Besides, his prices isn't as good as ours," Ace added.

"Just thought y'all should know what Stone on." Show and his two homeboys exited the spot.

Ace heatedly slammed his fist on the coffee table. "Stone got shit twisted if he thinks he gon' take us out the game," he spat.

"Havin' opps is part of the game so what we gotta do is make some more money so we can buy some more shooters," Chedda said as he tossed the stack of money atop the coffee table. "First we get the money, then we get the power, and then we get the respect."

"Fuck that. I'm talkin' 'bout ridin' out on Stone ass tonight."

"Let's just hit the club tonight and pop a couple bottles and pull a few bitches," Chedda suggested.

Ace knew they needed a night to unwind. "I'm down."

•••

Tonight the club was lit, and all Ace had in mind was poppin' bottles and leaving with a bad bitch. While walking through the club, Ace dapped up a few niggas and hugged several bitches he was familiar with. He was dripped in a tan Chanel sweater and black loose fit jeans with Chanel boots.

And Chedda was there rocking a Gucci sweat suit with Gucci sneakers. Usually they would pass on the club because they'd rather count money, but tonight they were at the club looking like money.

While Ace and Chedda stood rapping about their next re-up, some bad bitches stepped to them looking for a dance and a chance at coming up on a baller. Ace continued to chill and sip at his bottle of Rémy while Chedda took to the dance floor with the bitches. A sexy, coconut-complexioned bitch came strutting by Ace, wearing a body-hugging thigh-high red dress and nude stilettos, with her hair, nails, and brows on fleek. Shorty had nearly every nigga in the club admiring her phat ass.

Ace suavely grabbed her by the hand, stopping her in her tracks and said, "My name's Ace. And yours?"

"Coco." She thirsted after his good looks.

"Coco, how about you lemme buy you a drink." He flashed her a smile that she couldn't resist.

"As long as you'll also buy one for my homegirl," Coco replied.

"That's no problem."

Making their way over to the bar Ace ordered Coco and her thick-ass redbone homegirl drinks. He and Coco talked for a bit getting to know what each other's intentions were.

"Listen, how about you and your homegirl hit up the hotel with me and my nigga Chedda after the club," he offered.

Coco sipped at her glass of Hennessy. "I'm down. And I'm sure my girl won't mind, as long as your nigga ain't a bum."

"Me and my nigga are bosses who only fuck bad bitch-es."

"You can say that again!" Coco toasted with her homegirl and then they took a drink.

Once things were established with Coco and her homegirl, Ace went and found Chedda who was seated in the VIP section with some niggas from their hood. "Check it out, I got these two bad lil vibes lined up to spend the night with us at the telly," Ace told him.

"Cool. Just lemme know when you ready to bounce," Chedda said.

"I'ma go and piss out some of this Rémy, then we can bounce afterwards."

Ace made his way to the restroom which was occupied by several niggas. He overheard moans from a bitch who was apparently being fucked coming from one of the stalls. As he came to do, Ace stepped to one of the urinals and took a piss. He then washed his hands before heading out. Back in the restroom he'd gotten a bad vibe from a couple niggas, but maybe it was just the liquor.

Once Ace and Chedda had made it to the parking lot they each grabbed their poles from inside the Maxima, just in case. Ace texted Coco in order for her and her homegirl to meet them outside. Ace sparked up a blunt while Chedda was on the phone tryna give his BM an excuse as to why he wouldn't be able to come home tonight, and from the sounds of it, Ace could tell he was having a hard time convincing her. Ace knew Chedda's BM had him on a short leash. He himself was with Paris now, but Ace still kept his options open.

Being near closing time lots of the clubbers were beginning to exit the club and niggas were out there parking lot pimpin' on the bitches who flaunted their assets. Shortly thereafter, Coco and her homegirl stepped up finding Ace leaned back up against his whip and Chedda seated on its hood. "I see you smokin' good!" Coco said, referring to Ace blowing on the blunt of OG Kush.

Ace hit the blunt and then replied, "'Cause my money good. Anyway, this is my nigga Chedda. I'm sure he's right for your homegirl." He gave the redbone a once-over thinking she was bad, and Chedda slid off the hood of the car and began shooting his shot at her.

Suddenly, Ace peeped a hooded figure approaching with a purpose. And a moment too late he noticed there was a pistol being aimed at him by Bullet!

Boc, boc, boc, boc, boc, boc!

"Aaah!" Coco yelped. She and her homegirl hit the ground and bystanders scrambled for cover, hoping to avoid being struck by stray bullets.

Bullet busted at Ace with intent to kill. As Ace quickly took cover beside the Maxima, he pulled his Glock and Chedda ducked inside the car, all the while Bullet continued firing and Ace returned fire. It was no doubt that Bullet had shown up because he was tipped off about Ace being on the scene. Ace and Bullet shot it out wanting to smoke each other, flames from their barrels lit up the parking lot and slugs flew. During the shootout, Ace managed to pop Bullet in the neck and chest dropping him.

"Yo Ace, hurry and get the fuck in the car!" Chedda implored. He was seated in the driver's side with the engine running.

As Ace hurried for the car, a couple of other niggas began airin' out him and Chedda. They were actually the niggas whom Ace had gotten the bad vibe from back in the club's restroom, and obviously they'd been the ones to tip off Bullet. Chedda shot back at the niggas out the window as Ace jumped inside the car. Then Chedda peeled off before Ace could even shut the door, being that the Maxima was being peppered with bullets. Ace and Chedda kept their heads low to avoid being popped as they fishtailed out of the parking lot and away from the scene.

"Shit!" Ace cursed in pain. He hadn't realized he was shot in the arm.

"What's wrong?" Chedda wanted to know as he sped the whip through a yellow traffic light.

"The nigga popped me. I need to get to a hospital ASAP." He was bleeding all over the place.

"Say no more." Turning the whip eastbound, Chedda steered towards the nearest hospital. "That pussy-ass nigga need to be murked," he growled.

"I know I at least popped the nigga," Ace told him. "Damn, this shit burns!" He nursed his wounded arm.

Chedda tried to keep him calm and collected. "Nigga, now you gon' be finally respected," he cracked. Once Ace was to check into the hospital, Chedda knew Twelve would be all over him about his bullet wound. "You know the alibi, they started shootin' and we was standin' by. You ain't see nothin'," he told Ace.

Once at the hospital, Ace checked in at the emergency room center. Ironically, this was the same hospital he'd been rushed to after being popped by Bullet before. When he was seen the nurse gave him a shot of morphine in the arm which soothed the pain. His wound was superficial having traveled through and through. The nurse thoroughly cleansed the wound and stopped its bleeding. After stuffing the wound with gauze and wrapping it with a bandage, Ace was good to go. But due to protocol, the laws were informed and had shown up to question Ace.

"So, do you wanna tell me how'd you end up shot this time, Ace?" Detective Lucas pressed while his partner, Detective Bradshaw stood beside him wearing a scowl. It was good cop / bad cop from before doing the questioning, and instantly Ace reflected to Lucas assuring they would be seeing him again, whether dead or alive.

"Ain't see shit. I was just standin' by when the shootin' started," Ace told him.

"Cut the bullshit!" Lucas raved. "This time around your ass is in deep shit. You've already been identified as being involved in the reported shootout that took place at the club, by a wounded bystander."

"And on top of that, we're in the process of pulling the video footage as we speak," Bradshaw added much more assertively than he'd been before.

Ace knew better than to incriminate himself. "I wanna talk to an attorney."

"Listen here, you sleazeball, you're gonna tell us what we wanna know right this minute," Bradshaw pressed.

"No need to press him because we already have more than enough evidence to arrest him," Lucas told his partner. He turned to Ace and pulled out his cuffs. "For your information, the guy you shot back at the club was announced DOA. You're under arrest for first degree murder."

Martell "Troublesome" Bolden

Chapter 5

After the long, stressful process of being booked into the Milwaukee County Jail, Ace was escorted to a pod. It wasn't long until he was informed by a C.O. that he had an attorney visit. In a small, cold room, he met with a clean cut, nice suit and tie wearing, middle aged Black man, who rose to his feet to introduce himself.

"I'm your attorney, Willie Williams." He and Ace shook hands. They took a seat. "I met with your close friend earlier today concerning your legal matters. He and I have come to terms that I'll be representing you in the court of law."

"So, can I count on you to beat this case for me?" Ace wanted to know.

"You're being charged with murder. From my experience, those are some of the easier cases to beat, as long as you didn't make a statement incriminating yourself. However, as your representative, I can't guarantee you but one thing, I'll do my best in your favor throughout this case."

Ace felt a bit easier with the lawyer Chedda had gotten for him. It was hard on Ace facing a murder charge, so to have an attorney who would fight for his freedom was what he needed. Even still, Ace understood there was evidence against him and he was willing to take the murder charge to trial. He'd rather be the suspect than the fuckin' murder victim.

Williams leaned back in the plastic chair and folded his legs. "So, tell me in detail how everything transpired leading up to the murder."

"It's like this. We were in the club's parking lot just chillin' with some bitches when all of a sudden, the nigga came outta nowhere bustin' at me and hit me in the arm. So I upped my gun and bust back. Then we hopped in the car and

49

fled the scene. That's how it went," Ace explained and Williams jotted down notes. He didn't believe the attorney needed to know of the prior beef which led to the incident at the club so he wouldn't mention it. Because all that mattered was the details of the incident that landed him a visit with the attorney.

"So, you mean to tell me that the victim shot at you first, and even hit you, so you were protecting yourself?" Williams noticed the pink stained bandage wrapped around Ace's wounded arm.

"That's the way I see it. And the laws say there's even footage of it."

"As of now, I have yet to receive any evidence pertaining to this case. But rest assure that I will, and if there is footage showing exactly what you described, then we'll have some room to deal. While you have to be confined and go through the motions, I advise you to just be patient and not speak of your case to anyone else," Williams told him. "I'll work on helping you out of here.

•••

Ace's first few days in the county had him sick with it. He hated being surrounded with snake and rat niggas who were willing to jump on cases in the hopes of taking the stand in exchange for a time reduction. He didn't yet have a bail set, so he'd just have to sit it out as his case resolved. What bothered him most was that he didn't know how long he'd be locked up, or if he'd ever even walk free with the murder charge looming over his head.

There was a few niggas from Ace's hood in the pod with him. But he wasn't as tight with them as he was with Chedda. Unlike any of them, he trusted Chedda. He knew Chedda wouldn't snitch on him for shit. So when some of the niggas from the hood questioned about his case Ace would only say very little pertaining to it. Needing to clear his head, Ace made his way over to the tree of phones. He dialed Chedda on collect call.

"How you, my nigga?" Chedda answered.

"Stressin' and shit," Ace responded.

"Don't stress yourself over the case. Williams knows what he's doin'."

"It's not just the case that has a nigga stressin'. It's so many snitch-ass niggas around here that's willin' to jump on a nigga case. Niggas shouldn't be playin' the streets if they can't accept the what comes with it," Ace stressed.

"Facts," Chedda agreed. "You just keep it solid like a real one." He knew Ace was one to keep it real no matter what.

"As solid as a rock," Ace assured him. "So, what's goin' down in the streets?"

"My nigga, you just focus on gettin' back to the streets ASAP 'cause I need you out here."

"And if I have to, then I'ma do my time and not speak about nobody like a real one." Ace was real like that.

After a week in the county, Ace had a preliminary court hearing. During this hearing, the D.A. materialized the video footage of the incident and called a key witness to the stand that had been wounded during the shootout, who turned out to be the bitch Ace had met that night at the club, Coco. Apparently, Coco had been shot in the thigh by a stray bullet from Bullet's weapon. While on the stand, Coco gave her testimony.

The D.A., whom was a skinny white guy thinning at the top, stepped to the stand and narrowly eyed his witness. "Now, will you please point out the suspect you witnessed taking part in the murderous shooting," he told her. Of course, Coco pointed at Ace, and she could hardly look him in the face.

"Your Honor," Williams chimed in, "let the record reflect that my client is not guilty of this charge. And during trial we'll show and prove why he's not the suspect but the victim in this matter."

Immediately following the hearing, Williams and Ace met in order to discuss the pros and cons of Ace's case thus far.

"I've taken time to go over all of the evidence. And with several statements given by other witnesses and the video footage, at this point I'm pretty damn confident that I'm able to get your murder deemed justified," Williams informed, sure of himself. "And the testimony of the key witness during the hearing actually works in your favor, being that she testified that you only defended yourself after having your life placed in danger when the victim starting shooting first."

Ace liked the sound of what he was hearing. "So, how do you plan to get the murder deemed as justified exactly?"

"It'll definitely take me some wheeling and dealing, but I'll schedule a meet with the D.A. in order to discuss the facts I laid out to you, in the hopes of having him see things my way. If not, then we'll have to go to trial and beat the case. After all, we are dealing with the toughest D.A. in this district."

The D.A. handling Ace's case held a high conviction rate, primarily for murders. He was known to drive a hard bargain, if any at all. Also, he was one of the best at making the suspects seem guilty to the jury during trial. Although with all Williams had to work with, he stood a chance at convincing the hardcase D.A. Since his bail was set at a quarter million dollars during the preliminary hearing, now it was just a waiting process for Ace to find out whether his murder would be deemed justified or if he'd have to take that shit to trial.

•••

During Ace's wait period, aside from Mika and Chedda, he spent lots of his time bonding with Paris. She was proving to be down for him by paying him visits, accepting collect calls, and putting money on his books. In the two months he'd been on lock, Paris didn't miss a beat. Ace knew it takes a certain kind of bitch to hold a nigga down while on lock, because for most niggas as soon as Twelve put the cuffs on them, their bitch is gone.

"Ace," Paris said hesitantly. She was seeing Ace on a visit. "I, um, I gotta tell you something."

"What is it?" Ace wanted to know.

"I... I dunno what I'm gonna do without you." Tears began to fall down her cheeks and she peered down at her hands. "I need you... Our baby needs you."

Ace couldn't believe what he had just heard. "Paris, look at me. Are you tellin' me you're carryin' my baby?"

Paris nodded slowly. "I just found out I'm ten weeks along."

"Wipe your tears away and stop that cryin' and shit. Listen, no matter what, you gotta be strong. You can't be stressin' over me right now. You gotta focus on you and the baby. Paris, I never meant to get you involved in my street life."

"I can't fault you for the way you live, Ace. Now that we're having a baby, you should consider living differently whenever you come home," she told him.

In that moment Ace thought about potentially never getting out of jail to be there for Paris and the baby. He could only hope that somehow he would get around the murder case. One thing for sure, instead of snitch, Ace would rather do a life sentence.

Five months into his wait, Williams showed up at the county jail to see Ace. After bargaining with the hardcase D.A. on a few occasions, Williams finally got him to come to an agreement.

"I can tell you that it took some doing, but I managed to get the D.A. to deem your murder justified under one condition. In turn the deal is you'll have to plead guilty to possession of a firearm by a felon and accept three years imprisonment. Or, we can take our chances at trial, but if we lose then you'll be facing life in prison." Williams laid out the terms and conditions.

Doin' three years in prison beats doin' life, Ace contemplated. Not wanting to chance it, he said, "I'll take the deal."

The thought of having to be away from the streets for the next three calendars was tough on Ace. It had been established with Chedda that he would hold shit down while Ace was absent. He would leave Chedda with all of the product he had stashed away. As for Paris, she was less stressed knowing that Ace would be coming home sooner than later. She was now nearly six months pregnant and found out she'd be having a boy, which made Ace proud. He looked forward to going home to Paris and his son.

For now, Ace had to keep it solid. He'd do his time and not speak about that body like a real one.

Chapter 6

During Ace's bid a year, came and went. He spent most of his time talking on the phone, gambling, bustin' moves, and reading urban novels, all while awaiting his return to the streets. Not much had changed with him. He was housed in a medium-custody facility where a majority of inmates were only doing shorter bids. However, there was some radical activities taking place, but none which Ace couldn't handle. And in between the flashlight-cops and some jail-niggas, they made his time harder than it had to be. Although Ace did his time like a real one.

Aside from Chedda and Mika being there for Ace, he also had Paris holding him down. Things with he and Paris were kosher, she often brought their now nine-month-old son Adonis along to visit him. Adonis was the spitting image of his dad with his mama's complexion. Ace was proud to be the father of his son and, unlike his own father, Ace would be there for his seed when he got out of prison.

And whenever Ace rapped with Chedda, he kept Ace up on what was going down in the streets. Thus far Chedda had managed to get his money and weight up more. He still had Sly running the trap spots along with some young trappers pushing packs, including Glen. Not to mention, Chedda now had a team of young guns for the problems that came with more money, which he had been having more so with Stone, but nothing he couldn't handle.

As for Mika, Ace often called her collect. She kept him updated on her and Glen's status, who she said had jumped off the porch and landed in the streets. And she would tell him whenever Star asked about him, although she also told him that Star was fuckin' with the nigga Stone now.

Within the year Ace had been bidding a lot had changed in the streets.

Ace was housed in the cell with a nigga named T.Y., who was the type to talk about what he did for the streets, but Ace seen right through his façade. Ace didn't much like the nigga but chose to keep it cool. While he was laid back on the top bunk reading *A Gangster's Syn* by J-Blunt, interrupting his reading T.Y. came into the cell loudly gathering his things from the footlocker.

"Keep it down, I'm tryna read," Ace told him.

"This ain't no resort, it's prison. So if you don't like it then too fuckin' bad!" T.Y. remarked. He slammed the locker shut.

Ace jumped off the top bunk then stepped to him and snarled, "Nigga, watch your fuckin' mouth, or next time I'll hit you in it!"

"My bad, Ace. I didn't mean shit by it." T.Y. folded.

"Now get the hell out and leave me to my book." Ace climbed back up onto the bunk and went back to reading as he was left alone. He knew a nigga like T.Y. couldn't be trusted, so he would sleep with one eye open.

For the most part, Ace kept to himself. Because with the type of niggas around he found it hard to believe that most real ones are locked down as it's often said. The main nigga he could be found hanging around the institution with was Cain. He and Cain had known one another from around the streets, and now in doing their bids together they had grown tight. Ace fucked with Cain because like himself, Cain didn't talk about what he did for the streets, he just let the streets talk. Cain had been on lock for two years on a five-year stint for possession of drugs and gun charges. Brown skin with an average build and shorter dreads and tatts on his face, Cain was a trap nigga who would pop a nigga about his. And Ace planned to fuck with Cain once they were both back in the streets.

While sitting at a table in the day room, Ace and Cain was choppin' it up.

"A nigga can't wait to lay up in some pussy. But I ain't gon' let no pussy whip me," Ace commented.

"Yeah right, nigga!" Cain chuckled. "Pussy gon' be there when a nigga get the bag. Plus, there gon' be pussy-niggas lookin' to pull fuck shit."

"That's why a nigga gon' have to keep protection." Ace smirked.

"Fa sho."

Ace noticed a nigga named Steve-O making his way through the day room. The nigga owed Ace for a gambling debt from a card game of spades. Ace said, "Yo, Steve-O, when you gon' pay me what you owe?"

"As soon as we get commissary then I'll pay," Steve-O told him.

"You been sayin' that shit for two weeks now."

"Nigga, told you I'ma pay. But if you keep sweatin' me about it, then I won't pay you shit." Steve-O headed away towards the community restroom.

"I'm about to get down on this nigga," Ace told Cain. He hurried to his cell where he snatched the padlock off his locker, dropped it inside a sock, then stashed it on his person before making his way back to the day room. "Just lookout for me," he told Cain and then slipped into the restroom.

Ace found the restroom empty, aside from Steve-O who occupied one of the stalls, taking a shit. He pulled out the lock-in-a-sock as he approached the stall which he could see Steve-O's pants down around his ankles beneath it. Ace kicked open the stall's door and to Steve-O's dismay Ace came rushing in on him. As he bludgeoned Steve-O with the

57

weapon Steve-O tried blocking himself with his arms, but he was still busted up and swollen all over the head and face. Before hurrying out of the restroom, Ace stashed the weapon on his person and left Steve-O slumped on the toilet beat nearly to a bloody pulp.

"I'm sure now that nigga rather have paid his debt," Cain commented as he and Ace made their way towards their table in the day room.

"Bet his ass will next time." Ace smirked.

Ace had never gotten into any trouble for demonstrating on Steve-O, because Steve-O took what he had coming without complaint. However, niggas throughout the joint had gotten word that Ace was responsible for Steve-O's beating. Though it couldn't be proven Ace had done it there was one C.O. named Lash that figured Ace was the suspect. Lash had it out for Ace anyway, maybe that had something to do with jail-house snitches informing him that Ace was selling drugs on the compound. Ace would smuggle in drugs off the visit by swallowing balloons filled with substances and then he'd return to his cell and make himself hurl in order to retrieve the drugs. So every chance Lash got he would toss and search Ace's cell for contraband, but Ace stayed a step ahead of the flashlight cop by stashing his contraband inside bars of soap.

Ace was doing the time, he wasn't letting the time do him.

•••

Chedda had come to visit with Ace, which he rarely did. He had some news that was best to tell Ace in person being that the collect calls were subject to being recorded and monitored.

"How you?" Ace asked his boy.

"Never mind me. How you holdin' up in there?" Chedda inquired.

"You know me, still thuggin' and shit."

"Best not be in there lettin' niggas hoe you," Cheddar cracked.

Ace scoffed. "I do a lot of time on the yard with them gorillas and stand tall. Do I let niggas hoe me, quit bein' silly!"

"I expect nothin' less." Chedda smirked.

"Sure you didn't come here for that. So, what's the news?"

Chedda rested his elbows on the table. "Shit ain't lookin' good."

"How bad is it?"

"The feds did a sweep in the hood."

"Straight up?" Ace didn't expect to hear news of an indictment.

"Straight up. And they snatched up Baller and some of his boys from his crew. The worst part about it is the feds are still snatchin' niggas up under the RICO Act."

"And you don't know if you'll be one of 'em," Ace added. He could tell the sweep had Chedda spooked. "All they need is a reason to connect you to Baller's drug ring."

"So far I'm in the clear, and I need to keep it that way."

"Then you need to keep a low profile. Stay off the line and off the scene as much as you can for now," Ace advised.

"Will do."

"Chedda, I need you to stay in them streets."

"Trust, I ain't lettin' the feds take me out the streets so easy," Chedda assured. "Enough about that shit. You ready to get back to trappin' and dodgin' cases in nine months?"

"Been ready. Even if it comes with me possibly catchin' another bullet or another body."

"Just know that them streets ain't the same no more."

"I'm sure. I heard the nigga Stone in the streets gettin' it in." Chedda scoffed. "Word on the streets is Stone been havin' plugs offed so he could supply their hoods. Let his ass try me and I'ma fuck around and catch a body."

"I already wanna get at Stone's head, so if he try any of that shit with you then when I hit the bricks, I'ma take his head off his shoulders," Ace swore.

"Look, don't worry about Stone. I got shooters for niggas like him."

"Chedda, just make sure you do your all to stay alive and free in them streets."

"You just make sure you be ready to get it in when you touchdown."

Ace eyed Chedda and stated, "I'ma touchdown and cause hell."

•••

Outside on the courtyard, Ace and Cain posted near the basketball hoops, where they stood off to the sideline conversing while niggas were on the court hooping. Before Ace knew it, a group of three niggas drove on him with a purpose.

"You the nigga Ace, ain't you," the stocky nigga said as a statement more than a question. Ace didn't know the stocky nigga, but he remembered seeing him around the joint before hanging with his celly, T.Y., and as far as Ace was concerned, he and the stocky nigga didn't have shit to talk about.

Ace replied, "Yeah, that's me. Who wanna know?"

"R.I.P. Bullet, bitch-ass nigga!"

The stocky nigga took off on Ace, striking him square on the jaw. Ace instantly struck Stocky back. One of Stocky's homeboys jumped in and while Ace fought with both of them, Cain took off on the third nigga and was too busy thumping with him to assist Ace. The stocky nigga and his homeboy were beating Ace's ass badly, but he fought to stay on his feet in order to keep from getting stomped out. A buzzer sounded informing the C.O.'s there was a fight on the courtyard. A moment later, there were numerous C.O.'s on the yard with cans of mace and some with X-26 tasers to break up the brawl. Ace was maced and then tackled onto the pavement by Lash, and other C.O.'s broke up the rest.

During the fight Ace had taken a beating, his lower lip was busted and left eye swollen. And Cain had been shanked multiple times but would manage to survive. Apparently Stocky was homeboys with a dead Bullet and wasn't willing to let Ace slide. They were all hauled off to the hole.

The fight landed Ace in the hole for the next six months. While in the hole, Ace passed time by doing countless push-ups and sit-ups, and due to his routine workout he was physically fit. And he did lots of reading, mainly urban novels. He also wrote letters to Paris often since he was limited to only two collect calls monthly, and he looked forward to receiving her love letters in return smelling sweet of her perfumes which she sent along with sexy photos that he'd jack-off to with lust. Other than those things, he utilized his time in solitude to mentally prepare himself for what was bound to come once he returned to the streets.

Over the gallery, Ace often heard other inmates who were also in the hole. Some reminisced with other convicts about the free-world or discussed their plans for whenever they would get out of prison. Others could be overheard spitting raps back and forth or playing the imaginative game

"City" as a past time. Then there were those who couldn't help but be overheard lip-boxing and being disrespectful towards others. Not to mention some inmates often used their milk cartons to throw piss on C.O.'s that mistreated them in some way, Lash being one of them.

After a few months, Ace realized the hole was designed to break niggas, whether mentally or spiritually or both. So much so that during routine count time C.O.'s would find inmates with sheets tied around their necks attempting to hang themselves, and others would use sharp objects and attempt to cut main arteries, all to try and escape the harsh reality which they were subject to suffer for the time being. Some inmates would even go on hunger strike in the hopes of forcing the administration to change the horrible circumstances of solitary confinement. However, Ace didn't allow the adversity of the hole break him in any way, instead it built his character.

"Yo, Cain, how you holdin' up?" Ace called out over the gallery from behind the locked cell door.

"Like a real one," Cain replied. He was housed a few cells down on the gallery. "How you?"

"I'm standin' tall! A nigga just lookin' forward to gettin' back to them streets," Ace told him.

"You and me both. More than anything I look forward to bein' with my bitch Tia and our lil ones. She been holdin' a nigga down through this shit and deserves for me to keep shit real with her when I touch," Cain said. Tia was his longtime girlfriend whom he had three kids with, and he loved his family to death.

"I feel you, fam. I just don't know if I'm ready for all that settlin' down shit."

"My nigga, every thug needs somebody to settle down with. As long as a nigga ain't settlin' for less."

"Facts." Ace knew Paris was more than he could ask for in a bitch.

"At least a nigga bitch gon' love him, but the streets love no one. So you gotta be ready for all the hate in those streets that's gonna come your way," Cain forewarned.

"Once I'm back in the streets, on everything I love, I won't hesitate to pop a hater," Ace assured.

"Ace, just don't tell a soul what you did for the streets."

•••

After his six months in the hole was up, Ace returned to general population. By then he was down to three months until he was to hit the streets. And Ace was becoming anxious to get back to the money, although he knew it would come with problems.

Bringing along Adonis, Paris had come to visit Ace. He always looked forward to visiting with his girl and son. Paris was looking good and Adonis had grown a lot, he was walking and talking so much more. Ace loved them both so much, although he knew that once he got out, he would have to somehow balance his family life with his street life.

"Bae, I can't wait until you come home to us," Paris expressed.

"Me neither," Ace replied. He sat across from Paris with Adonis sitting on his lap, eating a bag of Cheetos purchased from one of the visiting room's vending machines. "Listen, I want you to know that not too much is gonna change with me when I'm back in the streets."

"Ace, you can't be serious right now. I can't believe you're still only thinking about yourself." Paris sounded deceived.

63

"Stop trippin' and shit. I'm sure this isn't what you wanna hear. Just know that whatever I do in those streets will be to make sure we're taken care of."

It was tough for Paris to hear Ace talk about getting back into the streets. She leaned back in her seat with her arms folded and huffed, "Whatever, Ace."

For the remaining of the visit Ace focused most of his attention on Adonis. He played some board games with Adonis and shared some junk-food with him that was purchased from the vending machines. Paris adored the sight of Ace interacting with his son, all she wanted was for him to be a family man when he came home. What Ace needed her to understand was that he would be there for her and his son because they meant so much to him, although it wouldn't prevent him from playing the streets.

Once a C.O. informed them their visit was over, Ace hugged Paris and noticed a tear creeping down her cheek. "What's the matter, Paris?" he inquired.

"I just don't want to see you go through any of what you already have again. Ace, next time you may not be so lucky to make it out of prison or make it out alive," Paris stressed.

"I can't tell you whether or not I'll go through some of the same shit. Just know that all I've been through has caused me to see shit different now. But the game don't change."

Ace was willing to accept the wins and losses that came with the game once he was back in the streets.

Chapter 7

Ace's three-year prison bid was finally over and he was back in the trenches. Prison wasn't shit that he couldn't handle, although he never again wanted to be living on a cellblock. So he wasn't against holding court in the streets.

Chedda had picked up Ace from the Racine Correctional Institution on his release date. He had brought Ace a Nike jogger outfit and a pair of Nike AirMax 360s to be released in, and he looked out for Ace with an iPhone and ten G's in his pocket. Ace knew that Chedda had gotten his money and weight up while he was doing his bid up north. And Chedda was only looking out for Ace because Ace would do the same for him. They were loyal to one another like that.

The two rolled foreign in Chedda's pearl white Audi A8 with tan leather interior and chrome twenty-four-inch rims. During the ride to their destination, Moneybagg Yo's "Cold Shoulder" played in the background as Chedda caught Ace up on what was going down in the streets, and Ace took heed to everything Chedda told him so he could be up to speed. Ace knew ever since Chedda had managed to dodge the indictment that Chedda played the streets differently.

"These streets ain't the same, Ace. Gotta be on point 'cause niggas out here finessin' shit, strippin' shit, murkin' shit, and snitchin' on shit over a lil bit of money. Plus, some bitches be in on the shit, so they ain't to be trusted," Chedda was saying.

"Sounds the same to me, because money has always been a motive to pull shit in the streets," Ace replied.

"The difference is now that our money right, we're the ones who niggas lookin' to pull shit on. Whether it be them pullin' a jack move or pullin' a trigga."

Ace shifted towards Chedda in his seat and told him, "I'm down for bein' in the trenches gettin' it in, Chedda."

"And I'ont doubt you down for whatever," Chedda assure him. He pulled to a stoplight on 27th and State Street. "Check it, when we get to the hood, I'ma make sure you get your sack right and a pole. You know it's back to the basics."

"Say no more."

"And I can't have you out here lookin' like you hurtin'. So we on the way to the barbershop now."

"Nigga gotta stay fresh as hell if the feds watchin'!" Ace smirked.

"Fa sho! Afterwards, I'll take you the mall and blow a bag on you a new wardrobe."

"That won't be necessary. My bitch Paris already cashed out on more than enough kicks and 'fits for a nigga," Ace told him.

Chedda pulled off with traffic. "Paris is a good bitch for you, my nigga. And she takes good care of your son. You gon' be with her now that you're out?"

"Bein' with Paris and my son is what I want. But I ain't with all the settlin' down shit."

"Nigga, you know Paris love your ass."

"Don't get me wrong, I love her too," Ace responded.

Chedda glanced over at him and said, "If you say so."

Ace really did love Paris and cared to be with her and his son. However, he knew that living the street life wasn't what she wanted for him, even though it was the only life he knew. While on their way, Ace decided to FaceTime Paris.

"Hey, baby! How long will it be until you come home to me and your son?" Paris said once she answered. She had Adonis on screen with her, who was excited seeing his daddy.

"Just give me a couple hours and I'll be there," Ace told her.

"Still don't understand why you didn't let me come pick you up." She shook her head. It took a lot of convincing to get her to let Chedda pick up Ace instead.

"I know you actually wanted to be the one to come pick him up from the institution. But it was best to let Chedda pick me up instead, so he and I could kick it before I come home to you and Adonis. Don't worry, Paris, y'all will have me all to yourselves whenever I get there. A'ight."

"Ace, just don't keep us waiting for long before bringing your ass home to us."

"Believe me, I wanna see you and my son as soon as I can. Plus, you know a nigga can't wait to smash your bad ass." Ace smirked.

"Then I'll be waiting on you." Paris offered him a sultry smile before they ended the call.

Ace looked forward to seeing Paris and Adonis. Though he had seen them nearly every weekend on visits and spoke with them nearly every day on collect calls while in prison, neither came remotely close to actually being able to go home to his girl and his son.

Arriving at the barbershop, Chedda parked the Audi at the curb. They went inside and Ace got his haircut. The barber gave him a low cut with a taper which complimented his brush waves. Plus, he'd grown a goatee.

After leaving the shop Chedda stopped at a liquor store in the hood. While Chedda stepped inside the store Ace stayed in the whip, and he noticed two niggas posted out front catchin' plays. Once Chedda returned to the whip with a box of blunts and bottle of Rémy, they were ready to head to the block. Suddenly a nigga came from around the corner with a gun in hand.

Boc, boc, boc, boc!

Both Ace and Chedda instantly ducked when the shots suddenly rang out. Chedda quickly pulled his .19 Glock with the thirty-shot clip from beneath his seat before he and Ace realized they weren't the targets. The gunman aired out the niggas posted in front of the liquor store.

"Nigga, let's get the fuck outta here before Twelve shows up!" Ace urged.

As Chedda peeled off he glanced over at Ace and said, "Shit still savage in these streets."

The streets were just as Ace remembered, filled with drug infestation and gun violence. Ace hadn't been out an entire day and already the streets were moving. He planned to make moves of his own in the streets over time.

Once they were on the block, Chedda parked before Mika's crib. Ace stepped out the car and then went inside the house to see his sister. He found Mika in the kitchen.

"Hey, bro! Glad you're finally out of jail," Mika exclaimed.

"Me too," Ace replied.

"Just make sure your ass stay out. But if I know you, you're getting right back into the game."

"Thing is I never got out of it."

"But now you have Paris and your son to think about."

"And I'ma be there for them. But I already let Paris ass know what I'm on."

"Bro, just try to do right by them."

"Fa sho," he assured. "Where's Glen, I wanna to rap with him."

"He's out there doing who knows what. Glen really has taken after you a lot. I just don't want nothing to happen to him in the streets," she stressed.

"Sis, a nigga never know what's gon' happen in the streets. He just gotta be willin' to accept it," Ace told her.

"Look, I just dropped by to see you real quick but I gotta get goin'." He hugged Mika before heading out.

When Ace stepped outside, he noticed Glen posted out on the block and nearly didn't recognize him. Glen now had long dreads, a gold grill, and tatts covering his arms. He was now eighteen and thuggin'. And he went by Gee.

"What's good, lil bro?" Ace greeted Glen with a thug-hug.

"It's good that you're back out here in these streets!" Glen said.

"It's only good for the niggas I fuck with." Ace smirked.

"Facts. Gotta be ready shake somethin' like my pit." Glen had with him a pitbull with a cocaine white coat of fur that he named Beast-Mode.

"Nigga, that bitch is a mutt." Ace laughed.

Glen roughed up the dog and it made a menacing growl and bark. "Beast-Mode is a killa!"

As Ace rapped with Glen a crack-head came along and Glen served the disheveled lady. Ace had always known Glen would jump off the porch, and now he was putting in work. And Ace would give Glen the game so he know what he's part of. While Glen was servin' the crack-head, Ace was approached by Neesha. She was with a homegirl that Ace didn't know, who was light-skinned with red hair. Ace expected to find Star with Neesha instead. He talked with Neesha briefly and she introduced him to the light-skinned bitch named Red, she had moved into the hood while Ace was on lockdown. Once Neesha's baby daddy pulled up, she stepped over to his car.

As Ace stood on the block, he was welcomed home by numerous residents from around the hood. The hood hadn't changed.

"Fucked up what happened with the nigga Baller," Ace said. He and Chedda were sitting on Mika's front porch drinking the bottle of Rémy.

"Word is one of Baller's own boys ratted him out," Chedda told him.

"So since Baller been indicted, you're servin' the hood now?" Ace sipped the bottle before passing it.

"For the most part. Stone serve a few niggas in the hood too. He even got some niggas he be frontin' work."

"On the real, Stone and whoever fuck with him can get it," Ace stated. "Anyway, since Baller has been indicted, who you coppin' weight from?"

"I'm coppin' weight from a Spanish guy named Shane. He be pluggin' me for the low. Plus, his product be pure cocaine, so I'm able to stretch it," Chedda told him.

"When the time's right, I'd like to meet the guy myself."

"Cool. I'm sure you two will take a likin' to each other."

Their discussion was interrupted by Neesha loudly fussing at her baby's daddy, Quincy. She followed closely behind Quincy, yelling as he headed for his car. Ace and Chedda were familiar with Quincy but they wasn't tight with him. The hood could always depend on Neesha to make a scene.

"You a good-for-nothin'-ass nigga! Always buying yourself new shit but never your kids!" Neesha raved.

Quincy spun on his heels and slapped her. "Listen, bitch, watch your fuckin' mouth and stop frontin' out here!"

Ace asked Chedda to see his pole and with no problem, Chedda pulled the .19 off his waist then handed it over to him. With the pole in hand, Ace walked by Red as he headed towards Neesha and Quincy. Ace struck Quincy over the back of his head with the gun, knocking him down onto the sidewalk. He then gripped Quincy by the shirt and repeatedly struck him across the face, beating Quincy bloody. After patting Quincy down and finding he wasn't strapped, Ace took all of the cash from Quincy's pockets and then handed it over to Neesha. Quincy managed to climb to his feet, stumbled to his car and then smashed off.

"That nigga crazy, girl!" Red gasped, referring to Ace.

Ace stepped back over to Chedda who was chuckling. He handed Chedda back the pole and grabbed the bottle of Rémy from him, then turned it up to his lips. Ace noticed that across the street, while seated out on his front porch, Reverend Johnson had witnessed the entire ordeal. Rev just shook his damn head and Ace knew he disapproved.

"See you still the same savage-ass nigga." Chedda grinned.

"Like you told me earlier, shit still savage in these streets," Ace responded with a smirk. "Check, it's about time I get home to Paris and my son."

"Then let's ride." They hopped into Chedda's Audi and went on their way. Chedda had made a quick stop around the corner at the trap spot where he stepped inside and then returned with a Nike drawstring bag and set it in Ace's lap and told him, "Now it's back to the money."

Ace looked inside the bag and found a Glock .9 with two thirty-shot clips, a quarter brick of coke, and twenty G's cash. He eyed Chedda and said, "And money is the motive."

Back in traffic, the windows were rolled down an inch while they smoked on a blunt of loud. YFN Lucci's tune "Way Up" played in the background. Though it was the fall season, it wasn't very chilly out.

Chedda lowered the volume on the music. "Fam, let's hit the strip club tonight," he suggested.

"Not tonight. I already have plans to spend my first night home with Paris and my son. Besides, I rather lay up in some pussy than just lust over some," Ace told him. He hit the blunt.

"Lemme find out Paris got you on lock," Chedda half-joked.

"Like I found out your girl got you on lock."

"Nigga, she knows what it is, so—" Chedda's words were cut short when he spotted the unmarked Dodge Magnum in the rearview mirror. "Shit. Twelve behind us."

Checking the rearview mirror himself, Ace recognized who the unmarked detect car belonged to. "It's those crooked-ass cops, Lucas and Bradshaw. Them pigs stay up to no good." He disliked the two D's as much as they disliked him.

Chedda continued to drive real smooth and Ace kept cool. They were riding dirty with guns and drugs, and with them being young and Black and riding in a luxury vehicle, they were subject to be pulled over. Ace knew his boy well enough to know if the D's tried pulling them over for a traffic stop, Chedda would take them on a high-speed chase. Besides, Ace wasn't willing to go back to prison under any circumstances, even if he had to go out bustin'. Luckily the unmarked Magnum just switched lanes and passed by them in traffic.

They pulled to the curb before the apartment complex. Ace let Chedda know he'd get with him tomorrow and they shook up, then Ace grabbed the Nike bag and stepped out the whip. Before riding off, Chedda waved at Paris who was standing at the entry of the complex with Adonis. He'd grown familiar with them during Ace's absence because he had looked after them. Adonis scurried up to Ace and he scooped Adonis up in his arms. With a joyful smile Paris ambled towards Ace and they embraced.

"A nigga couldn't wait to come home to y'all," Ace said.

"And we couldn't wait to have you home either," Paris replied.

Adonis grabbed Ace's face and said, "You gonna stay at home with us now, Daddy?"

"Yeah, and I ain't goin' nowhere."

They entered the apartment. Ace instantly felt at home, he admired how the place was plushly furnished. Not to mention, the aroma of a home cooked meal wafting in the air. Adonis eagerly wanted Ace to come see his room and Paris went into the kitchen to finish prepping the meal. But first, Ace headed to the master bedroom in order to stash away the goods he received from Chedda because he didn't want Paris to know he was already up to no good. He placed the Nike bag inside the closet.

"Bae, what are you doing?" Paris asked.

Ace turned and found her standing near the door. "Just checkin' out the place."

Paris walked up on him and wrapped her arms around his neck. "So, how does it feel to be back home?"

"Like this is where a nigga belongs."

"Well, me and Adonis need you here with us." Paris lifted on her tiptoes and pecked him on the lips. Reciprocating, Ace palmed her plump ass and tongue kissed her. "Boy, stop before you start something. Save it for later. You better come on because your bad-ass son is in there waiting for you."

They had enjoyed the meal like a family. Afterwards, Adonis had fallen asleep in Ace's lap while they watched TV. Ace carried his son into his own bedroom and laid him in bed while Paris watched with adoration. The two stood at Adonis's bedside and took a moment to watch him sleep soundlessly. Ace then wrapped his around Paris's small waist and pulled her close to him and the two shared a passionate kiss. It had been a long time since they were able to have each other in every way.

Paris took Ace by the hand and led him into their bedroom. She then began to help him out of his clothes and he returned the favor. They explored each other's bodies, hers curvy and his chiseled. Ace's dick was hard. He turned Paris around and bent her over the edge of the king-size bed, then slid into her pussy from behind. Paris had kept it tight for Ace while he was on lockdown, aside from the occasional one-night stands. Her pussy was much better than he had remembered, and far better than fuckin' his own hand. He slid his dick back and forth in her wetness, enjoying the feel of how tight the pussy was.

"Damn, bae, this shit feels so good," Ace grunted as he dug her out. Her moans of pleasure encouraged him to fuck her harder.

"Yes, Ace! Oooh... that's my spot, baby!" Paris moaned. She looked back at it while Ace gripped her ass and hit her spot with each stroke.

"Who pussy is this, huh?"

"Yours, baby! Yours!"

Ace busted a nut. He pulled his dick out of her snatch and released his semen on Paris's ass. Paris turned and kissed Ace, slipping her tongue inside his mouth. She pushed Ace back on the bed and then she climbed on top and straddled him. Her wetness slid down on his hard dick. Ace palmed her ass and slammed her up and down on his hardness. She liked looking him in his eyes while she rode him. Her breasts jiggled as she bounced on Ace's dick.

"Uhmmm... This dick feels amazing, baby!" Paris cried out in pleasure. She felt herself about to cum and crawled up and straddled Ace's face. "Eat me until I cream in your mouth," she urged. Ace tasted Paris's juices once she lowered her pussy onto his mouth. He licked her slit, flicking his tongue over her clit. Paris's back arched as Ace hungrily ate her pussy. She tossed her head back, enjoying the feel of him orally pleasuring her. Her body began to convulse as she came, and Ace loved how her juices oozed into his mouth.

Paris slid down and then sucked on the tip of Ace's dick. She twirled her tongue around its swollen head and then slipped it inside her mouth down to the base. While gazing up into Ace's eyes, Paris licked the shaft of his dick then sucked his sac. The feeling of her swirling his balls around in her mouth drove Ace wild!

"Shit Paris, you doin' that," Ace groaned. Paris stroked his dick with her hand while she flicked he tongue over its tip. Ace palmed the back of her head and guided her warm, wet mouth up and down on his dick. As Paris sucked the dick like a beast, Ace's toes curled and he bust a nut in her mouth, which she swallowed every drop of.

They lie in bed silently enjoying the presence of one another. Ace lay on his back and Paris rested her head on his chest. He lie awake while she eventually fell asleep. Ace was lost in thought, he couldn't help but think of the money, drugs, and gun he had stashed away in the closet. *First day out of prison and already I've taken penitentiary chances*, he contemplated. But those were the chances he was willing to take, and he'd accept the consequences that came with them.

Peering down at Paris took his thoughts to her and Adonis. He loved them both to death, which is why he had no problem putting his life on the line for them. Paris had never been one to give a damn whether he was rich or poor, she loved him for who he was. And he loved her just the same. Ace would do his all to be a better dad to his son than his own dad was to him, and all that would take is for Ace to be there for Adonis.

Ace wanted to be there for Paris and Adonis both. Although he understood that the trenches could take him away from them at any given moment, whether it be prison or death.

Chapter 8

The streets hadn't changed much and neither had Ace. It had been six weeks since his return to the streets and he'd been trappin' hard. Over time he'd managed to come up off the yae Chedda hit him with and now, not only was Ace working with yae, but he also had loud. Ace was working with a half brick of yae and three pounds of loud, and he'd stacked nearly thirty more G's. Also, he kept his ears to the streets, hearing of niggas who were rats and snakes that were to be avoided. And Ace made sure to keep the pole on him when he moved through the streets, he'd rather be caught dead with it than without it.

While in the trap, Ace and Glen were playing NBA2K on PlayStation, and Chedda was in the kitchen cookin' up crack. Now Glen was around regularly, and Ace actually liked having him around, because not only was Glen about his riches but he was savage with his.

Ace's iPhone rang and he scooped it up from the end table, cradling it in between his ear and shoulder while still handling the joystick. "S'up, bae?" Ace answered, knowing it was Paris.

"Hey. I'm calling to remind you that I go on lunch break in a bit and I don't want you to forget to bring me lunch," Paris told him.

"I remember, bae. You want me to bring you a KFC famous bowl with a pink lemonade. I'm on my way now."

"And make sure you hurry your black self up," she insisted before they hung up the call. Ace knew she was pointing out his tardiness. Just this morning he had made her twenty minutes late to work.

Tossing on his Air Jordan's, Ace was finna go and take his girl lunch. "Gee, we'll have to finish this game up later.

Yo, Chedda, I'll be back in a minute," Ace told his boys. He grabbed his pole from the end table and placed it on his waist before slipping into his leather Pelle Pelle jacket. Then he bounced.

Ace rolled in Paris's white Honda Accord. He didn't have his own ride at the moment, but it wouldn't be long before he copped himself one. For now he'd use his girl's ride to get around. Ace stopped at the nearest KFC en route to Paris's workplace. Instead of using the drive-thru, he chose to park and walk in to place his order. He thought the drive-thru seemed to make easy targets out of anyone for lurking jackboys and shooters. After placing his order and receiving the food, he was on his way. Steering the ride with one hand, he used the other to eat a piece of chicken. Needing to wash down the chicken, he took a few sips of Paris's drink.

Arriving at the daycare where Paris worked, Ace parked out front. He sent her a text that he was outside. While awaiting Paris, he removed the .9 from his lap and placed it beneath his seat, knowing she didn't care for him to be back totin'. Of course, she knew he was back at it in the streets, although he tried not to bring his street affairs around her or his son. And Paris never complained much at all about his street life, unless she felt it was necessary.

A moment later, Paris made her way to the car and stepped into the passenger seat. "Ace, you're so messy," she pointed out, seeing that he had chicken grease on his fingers and around his mouth. She grabbed a napkin and wiped his mouth clean. Then she grabbed her food and drink and noticed the drink partially empty. "Ugh, Ace, your greedy-ass always do that!" she huffed.

"Do what?" Ace feigned ignorance.

"Dude, you know exactly what." She leaned over and pecked his lips, then said, "You best not be late picking up your son and me later on, Ace."

"Don't worry. I won't be," he assured before she went back into work and he smashed off.

As Ace steered back towards the trap house, he got a text message from Chedda to pick up a box of blunts and sandwich bags. He made a stop at the liquor store in the hood. Before stepping out the car, Ace positioned the pole inside the pocket of his jacket. Heading towards the store, Ace was stopped by a young boy who lived around the hood.

"S'up Ace? Will you buy me a blunt?" the young boy named Lil Cam asked. Being only fourteen, he wasn't old enough to buy his own blunt.

"A'ight, lil homie," Ace told him. Lil Cam tried offering him the money for his blunt and Ace declined it. "No need. I got you."

Inside the liquor store Ace impatiently stood in line while there was a chick at the register slowing the pace as she dug inside her knock-off Chanel handbag for change to pay for her items. Ace took it upon himself to speed up the process. He stepped up to the register and dropped a twenty on the counter. "Gimme a box of Swisher Sweets blunts and sandwich bags. Plus, I'm payin' for her," Ace told Abdul, who always was stoked to see him.

After receiving the items Ace told Abdul to keep the change and stepped outta the store. Ace pulled out one of the blunts from the box and handed it to Lil Cam and gave him his number to hit him up whenever Lil Cam wanted to cop some weed. As Ace headed for the Accord, the chick from inside the store stopped him in his tracks.

"Thought you should have this." The chick, whose name was Savvy, smiled and held out his receipt with her name and number scribbled on it. Once Ace accepted the receipt, she told him, "Feel free to hit me up whenever."

"Fa sho," Ace replied, wearing a smirk. He admired her ass when Savvy turned for her silver Chrysler Sebring. She hopped in then brought the engine to life and Megan Thee Stallion's "Savage" blared from the speakers as she pulled off down the street.

Ace had to admit that shorty was a bad lil vibe, although that didn't mean she was worth him cheating on Paris with. He saved her name and number in his iPhone for future reference as he stepped into the Accord.

Ace pulled to the curb and parked across the street from the trap house. He noticed Chedda standing out on the porch smoking a cigarette while talking into his iPhone. Chedda wore no jacket, bearing the chilly weather and it was cold enough to see his breath fog in the air, although snow had yet to fall. No matter the weather, trap niggas could be found posted up on the block catchin' plays. Stepping out the car, Ace grabbed the brown paper bag containing the items he'd picked up at the liquor store and then he walked towards the trap.

"A'ight, I'ma be outside waitin' on you," Chedda was saying to whomever was on the other end of the line as Ace stepped up on the porch. Chedda ended his call and took pull on the cigarette. "You pick up the blunts and bags?" he asked Ace.

Ace handed him the brown paper bag. "There you go."

Shortly thereafter, a black Dodge Intrepid pulled to the curb before the trap. Ace didn't recognize the car and he couldn't see inside past the tinted windows. He clutched the pole on his waist, not knowing what to expect. Evidently, Chedda knew the occupants of the Intrepid being that he waved for them to come inside the trap house. Three niggas emerged from the Intrepid, none of which Ace recognized. Chedda led them inside the trap, and Ace took up the rear. In the front room, Ace stood off to the side with the butt of his pole and its extended clip protruding from his waist and Glen was seated on the couch with his pole lying across his lap, both of them were on point while Chedda dealt with the niggas.

"So, what'll it be?" Chedda asked.

"A four-and-a-split," one of the niggas whose name was Jay requested.

Chedda knew he meant four and a half ounces. "That's gonna run you four G's."

Handing over a bankroll, Jay said, "It's all there."

After counting the paper and making sure it was good, Chedda weighed up the work on a digital scale atop the coffee table in front of Jay and his boys. He tossed the work into sandwich bags then handed it to Jay. "Just hit my line whenever you ready to re-up," Chedda told him.

"Fa sho." Jay and his boys exited the trap house.

Ace peeped out from behind the window blind and watched Jay and his boys load into the Intrepid then roll away. He turned to Chedda and stated, "I get a bad vibe from those niggas."

"Jay been coppin' work from me for a while now. He spends good money," Chedda responded. He began to roll up a blunt of loud.

Ace mused, *all money ain't good money.*

•••

Later in the evening, seated on the couch in the trap watching *Belly* with his boys, Ace's iPhone chimed, indicating he had a text. He scooped up the phone from the end table and saw the message was from Paris. Touching its screen, he read the text.

PARIS:
Bae I'll be working overtime so don't worry about picking me up until 6 pm. Just be sure to come pick up your bad-ass son on time.

He had to be there to pick up Adonis from daycare in an hour, and he'd have to be with him until Paris got off work. Ace replied with a text message.

ACE:
A'ight, I'ma be on time picking up my son. Me and him will kick it until you get off work.

PARIS:
Don't have Adonis in those streets with you. I prefer you either be at home with him or drop him off at Mika's place.

ACE:
He'll be good with me for a few hours. Stop trippin' n shit. Be there soon.

Ace never minded having his son along with him, although Paris worried whenever Adonis was out and about in the streets with him. Paris would always stress that she didn't want Adonis being influenced by seeing any bad things at his age, because she knew Ace would have him around drugs and guns and who knows what else.

An hour later, Ace had picked up his son. It wouldn't be long before Paris was to get off work. Since being home, he barely got the chance to spend time with Adonis, due to him frequently trappin' hard. Adonis rode in the passenger seat while Ace had taken him along as he caught a few plays. Then Ace stopped at McDonald's and purchased Adonis a Happy Meal. Adonis had only taken a few bites of his burger and fries, leaving the remaining of the food alone while he played with the toy that came with the Happy Meal. Ace was used to him doing that shit. Pulling to a stop at a stoplight on 27th and Wells Street, Ace gripped the pole lying in his lap. He checked his surroundings for cops and robbers, just being vigilant.

"Daddy?" Adonis called and Ace peered over at him. "That's yours?" He pointed at the gun.

Ace reached over and planted a hand on his boy's back. "Son, let me learn you somethin'. Yeah, this is mine. But this don't make me a man. What makes me a man is takin' care of you and your mama. A'ight?" he told him. Then he placed the gun beneath his own seat, because he didn't want his son thinking playing with guns was alright.

Once six pm came, Ace and Adonis were outside the daycare awaiting Paris to get off from work. Paris made her way out to the car and then entered the passenger seat. She leaned over and pecked Ace on the lips and then Adonis on the cheek, who was strapped into his car seat in the back. Ace pulled off in traffic.

"Adonis, you have fun with your daddy?" Paris asked.

"Yup." Adonis nodded his head.

"That's good."

Adonis added, "And Daddy got a big ol' gun!"

Paris glared over at Ace, who just shook his head as he steered the car towards their crib.

Martell "Troublesome" Bolden

Chapter 9

Done with having to use Paris's car, Ace went to the used car lot and copped himself an Acura TSX. The Acura was navy blue and in good condition, it was just a vehicle for him to trap in. He'd taken it to the neighborhood mechanic Mitch's home garage to make sure it was running properly. And Mitch came cheap being that he was an alcoholic and addict. Once the Acura was running properly Ace had taken it to the car shop to have its windows tinted and a sound system installed. Ace planned to pull out something else in time, but for the time being the Acura would do.

Being that it was now January, the winter season had taken its course, and Ace planned to stack his cash all winter so he could pull out when the summertime hit. With the weight he and Chedda was coppin' from Shane, Ace fronted more of his share of the yae than he actually moved on his own. Lately, he moved loud more so than yae. He was gettin' to the bag.

Pushing the Acura through traffic, Ace was on his way to catch a play with Glen riding along. He could be found hangin' with Glen more frequently than Chedda lately.

"I trust Chedda and all, but I just gotta meet this Shane guy for myself," Ace was saying.

Glen glanced over at him. "Think Shane's no good or some shit?"

"Not even. Just wanna know who we're dealin' with. And finally I'll get to meet Shane tonight." Ace was to go with Chedda to meet with Shane later on.

Once Ace's iPhone rang, he peeped down at it which was positioned in the cupholder, and he noticed on its display that the call was from Cain. After Ace was released from prison, he stayed in touch with Cain, who would call him collect. Whenever Cain called, Ace would keep him posted on as much as he could over the phone. Ace thought Cain was a real one and planned to get money with him once Cain touched down in less than a year. Ace accepted the call, which connected to the Acura's Bluetooth.

"S'up, my G?" Ace said.

"Still doin' my time like a real one," Cain replied.

"No doubt. You straight on bread, I can drop more off to your girl if you want."

"Won't be necessary. The bread you last gave her to send me is more than enough to hold a nigga over. Anyway, how shit comin' along for you in those trenches?"

"Just been trappin' so hard to get my money and weight up, all while duckin' haters and cops. However, I'ma be way up soon enough." Ace bent the car onto Concordia Street.

"Just make sure you stand on yours, 'cause niggas would like to catch you slippin'," Cain told him. "You totin'?"

"Fa sho. Glock .9 with a thirty." Ace's pole lay across his lap. "Plus my lil bro totin'," he added, referring to Glen and the Glock .40 he carried.

Cain chuckled. "I can't be totin' no handguns, unless that bitch come with a thirty. Maybe you need to get yourself a Draco," he suggested. After fifteen minutes the collect call ended, but not before Ace and Cain said their parting words.

Pulling to the curb in front of the run-down duplex home in the hood, Ace phoned Red who'd asked him over so she could purchase some loud.

"I'm outside," Ace told Red once she answered.

Red sucked her teeth. "Nigga, stop acting like you too damn good to come on in. The door's unlocked," she replied.

Ace and Glen stepped out the Acura and headed upstairs of the duplex home where Red stayed with her lil sister and mother. Also, Neesha was there, doing Red's hair in the kitchen. Glen conversed with Red's lil sister, Kiki, who didn't look all that young for her age. And neither did Red, who was only seventeen. Red was light-skinned with a voluptuous figure, although she wasn't the cutest chick in the flock. And it was obvious to Ace that Red was feelin' him, although he stayed shooting her down.

Red handed Ace fifty bucks in exchange for an eighth of loud. "Why don't you chill and match a blunt with me," she suggested.

"Maybe some other time. A nigga have some shit to tend to," Ace said and shot her down as usual. He pulled out a bankroll and folded the fifty bucks into it.

"Boy, look at you with all that damn money!" Neesha chimed in. She went on with her usual gossiping. "So, my baby daddy, right, he been talkin' shit about you, Ace. Talkin' 'bout whenever he catch you, he gon' fuck you up so you better watch your back and shit. His ass just mad that you treated him."

Ace wasn't one to do much back and forth, fuckin' with him a nigga gettin' popped. He lifted his shirt just enough to display the pole protruding from his waist and evenly responded, "I stay strapped."

Back in traffic, Ace and Glen was smoking a blunt while on the way to catch another play. Ace had gotten a call from one of his plays for an ounce of yae. Now that Ace was moving loud along with yae, his phone was constantly blowin' up, and on a good day he'd bag four, five G's off his phone. Getting his money and weight up was his objective.

"Seen you all over Kiki back there," Ace commented as he steered through traffic with Lil Poppa's "Real One" playing in the background at a modest volume.

"Yeah, she's just a lil freak that I be fuckin' on," Glen responded. He puffed on the blunt. "Nigga, I see Red was all over you. Why you shoot her down?"

"Ain't got time for a thot like Red. Anyway, Neesha told me Quincy's soft-ass talkin' 'bout I better watch my back. Yeah, right." Ace scoffed.

"I'd smoke that nigga if you want."

Ace shook his head no. "There are other niggas that can get the smoke. Like Stone."

"I'ont like Stone or his crew any-fuckin'-way. Just let me know and I'ma bomb on his ass." Glen and his miniature gang already had smoke with Stone's young guns around the hood over territorial purposes. So he wouldn't hesitate to burn Stone or any nigga who fuck with Stone.

"Leave smokin' Stone to me," Ace told him. "Speakin' of, nigga, pass the smoke." After taking another puff of the blunt Glen passed it to Ace.

Arriving at the destination, Ace pulled the Acura to the curb before an apartment building. As he was finna step out the car his phone rang, Ace noticed the call was from Chedda. He asked Glen to go and make the serve while he answered the call, and Glen obliged. Tucking the .40 on his waist and grabbing the work, Glen stepped out the car and then headed towards the apartment building to catch the play. Ace remained inside the car and answered the call.

"Damn, Ace, why is your ass late pullin' up on me?" Chedda complained.

"Just gimme a minute, I'm on the way," Ace replied.

"A'ight nigga, make sure you get here ASAP so we can go and meet up with Shane."

"Say no more. I'll—" Ace's words were intervened once he heard the sounds of shots erupting from inside the building. He was sure it was Glen involved in the shooting.

"Look, Chedda, I think some shit goin' down with Gee so I gotta go!"

"Then go ahead and check it out."

"Already," was all Ace said and then ended the call without warning before he jumped out the car with the .9 on his waist.

Glen came rushing out with his pole in hand as Ace was headed for the building. "Dawg, let's get the fuck outta here!" Glen urged. The two immediately jumped back into the Acura and sped away.

"Fuck went down back there?" Ace wanted to know.

"The nigga tried to poke me, so I upped and popped off."

Ace figured it must have been a set-up all along. "Did you pop the nigga?"

"Yeah, I did. Although I'ont know if I offed his ass." Glen was collected.

"Look, I'ma drop you off at the trap spot in the hood. You just lay low there." After Ace dropped off Glen, he went on his way to get up with Chedda. He parked behind Chedda's Audi in front of his apartment located out in the meadows and then Ace sent Chedda a text that he was outside. A moment later, Chedda made his way out then the two hopped into his Audi and headed to meet with the plug.

"Exactly what went down with Gee, is shit a'ight?" Chedda wanted to know as he dipped around a vehicle in traffic.

"Apparently, a nigga I had Gee serve tried to strip him, and Gee popped the nigga up," Ace answered.

Chedda glanced over at him. "The nigga dead?"

"Don't know. If not, I'ma dead his ass for tryin' me. Obviously, it was a set-up and instead it was supposed to be me the nigga strip."

"Just make sure you don't let no beef get in the way of gettin' to a bag," Chedda advised.

Ace shifted towards him. "Chedda, I'ma get the bag, you can put some trust on it. Been frontin' out most my work, so I'ont have to do much besides collect my proper chop. And I ain't takin' no shorts. I'm just tryna get my sack and bag right."

"And that's where Shane comes in at."

"Look, if Shane checks out, then we'll continue to fuck with him."

Ace and Chedda had been invited as VIP guests to the night club by the plug, Shane. Since Ace had been out of prison, he hadn't stepped a foot inside a club after his last experience there, which made him cautious about club scenes. However, Chedda convinced Ace to come along in order to meet the plug.

Inside the club, they were located in the VIP section, courtesy of Shane. He was a dark brown, short and stubby guy with a long ponytail and was mixed with Black and Mexican. Only in his late twenties, Shane was having money and playing with bricks of cocaine. He was plugged with the MS-13s, and anyone acting against them is dealt with quickly and with extreme violence. Although he was the suave type, Shane was not one to take lightly.

Seated on the red leather sofa, Shane sipped from a bottle of Ace of Spade. He was surrounded by his MS-13 crew and a crowd of bad bitches. Chedda sat beside him and Ace was across from them. While Chedda talked with the plug, Ace perpetually checked the surroundings. Everything seemed as it should be, niggas popped some bottles and made it rain, while bitches popped their pussies and raked it up. Everyone but Ace seemed to be enjoying themselves.

Rich $avage

"Ace, you need to chill, homes," Shane suggested. He grabbed a bottle of Dom P. from the bucket of ice positioned on the table. "Why don't you have yourself a bottle on me?" "Trust me, we're all good in here," Chedda assured him. "No doubt," Ace responded and accepted the bottle. Chedda noticed a nigga he conducts business with. "Gimme a minute, I see someone I need to get with." He stepped away to rap with the nigga, leaving Ace and Shane alone.

"Chedda tells me you're a good dude," Shane said.

"He tells me the same about you," Ace replied and then turned the bottle up to his lips.

"So, why'd you wanna meet me for yourself?" He eyed Ace inquisitively.

"'Cause I wanted to know the guy we're dealin' with, is all."

"Well, Ace, I think it's best you know who you're dealing with in this line of business. Because that way you'll know what kind of guy he is."

"All due respect to Chedda, just know I do things my own way," Ace told him.

"And I feel you on that, homes. I can see you're a real nigga, and as long as you keep it that way, I'll see to it you get rich." Shane sipped from his bottle. He whistled a bad-ass Latina bitch over and she sat on his lap.

"Keepin' it real is all I know," Ace replied coolly.

After parting from the club, Chedda pushed his Audi through traffic with Ace beside him. They pulled to a stop at a stoplight on 35th and Hampton Street. At a lowered volume, Tee Grizzley's "Trenches" played in the background.

"So, what you think about Shane?" Chedda wanted to know.

"Nothin' against Shane, I just don't think he's as good of a plug as Baller used to be," Ace admitted.

"Ace, Baller's old news and now we're who he used to be. So now it's on us to flood these streets. And as long as we fuck with Shane, then he'll give us weight on consignment and we'll make more money than you can count!" Chedda exclaimed.

"A'ight. But we both know more money means more problems. And I'm down to solve any that comes our way," Ace told his boy.

"Then niggas best not want any problems with us."

Chapter 10

Ace made a stop at Cain's girl, Tia's place. Tia lived in a low-income apartment with their three kids. She was the kind of bitch who relied on government assistance or a nigga to take care of her, instead of getting off her ass and finding herself a job. Not to mention, she was into clubbing more than a mother of three should be. Cain had been with Tia since they were teens and Cain loved her unconditionally, though Ace thought Cain could do better.

Once Ace knocked on the apartment door it opened a moment later, with one of the kids standing there with nappy hair and a snotty nose, wearing dirty clothes with his shoes on the wrong feet. Ace figured the lil boy was about the same age as Adonis. *Tia's ass need to be checked for allowin' her kids to look so damn bummy*, he thought.

"Oh, hey. Come on in," Tia said once she showed up at the door. She only wore a tank-top with no bra and a pair of short-shorts. Brown-skinned, short, and thick in all the right places, Tia was a pretty girl. Tia stepped aside, allowing Ace to enter the unkept place. "You can have a seat," she offered.

"I only stopped by real quick to drop off some cheese and pics for you to send Cain," Ace told her. He then fished out a bankroll and off three-hundred bucks and handed the cash, along with some pictures taken at the club to Tia. "Just make sure you send him that ASAP."

"I will," Tia assured. As Ace went for the door she stopped him and stepped into his personal space. "Ace, you can stay and keep me company, if you'd like."

"I'm good on that, Tia," he declined. "Whenever Cain calls, tell him I stopped by." He then exited the apartment.

Pushing the Acura on his way to the hood, Ace phoned Chedda to see what he was on for the night.

"A nigga stuck in the crib with BM and the lil ones tonight," Chedda told him.

"How 'bout I just come through and chill?" Ace asked.

"I'll just get with you tomorrow. Try to stay outta trouble until then."

"Fa sho."

Ace then phoned Glen twice and got no answer. He figured Gee was laid up with some bitch. Tonight he'd be riding solo. Reaching the hood, Ace stopped at the liquor store where he went inside to purchase himself a blunt. On his way out, he bumped into a heavier nigga. "Phat?" Ace recognized the nigga as Baller's right-hand man. After Baller had been snatched up by the feds, Ace figured Phat would've been also. However, Phat happened to duck the fed sweep.

"What's up, lil homie?" Phat shook up with him. "Last I heard you fucked around and caught a body," he said.

"Yeah, and I beat the body like Rocky."

"Enough said. Check it out, why don't you take down my number and get with me sometime. I'm sure we can be beneficial to each other in one way or another."

"Sounds good." Ace produced his iPhone and saved Phat's number before going on his way. As he stepped into the Acura, his phone began ringing and he answered as he started up the whip.

"Hey, Ace. Will you bring me an eighth of loud?" It was Red.

As Ace pulled off he told her, "I'm on the way."

Shortly thereafter, Ace parked at the curb before Red's place and texted her that he was outside. A moment later, she hastily made her way through the cold night winter weather and into the warmth of the Acura's interior behind tints.

"Ace, why do you always act like you too damn good to come into my house?" Red inquired, displaying attitude.

"Shorty, it ain't even like that," Ace answered coolly.

Red sucked her teeth. "Whatevs. Boy, where's my loud at?" She exchanged fifty bucks for the sack of weed. Noticing the blunt in the cupholder, Red grabbed it and insisted, "Smoke a blunt with me."

"A'ight. But I'ma roll up." Ace needed to get high any-damn-way.

YFN Lucci's "No Ceilings" played at a lowered volume while Ace and Red blew on the blunt of loud. They made small talk and even shared a couple laughs. The weed took its course and the two were high as hell barely halfway through the blunt. Ace puffed the blunt once more and then passed it to Red.

"Shorty, I'm finna ride out," Ace said. Checking the time, he saw it was nearly ten pm.

"Damn, you really just finna ride out on a bitch like that?" Red sounded disappointed. "Boy, you stay actin' like you're too good for me." Ace knew she wanted him.

"I told you, it ain't even like that."

"Hope not."

Ready to fuck right where they were parked, Red slid a hand in between his legs, grabbing at his dick. She'd been wanting to give him some pussy for the longest, and Ace was tempted. Red pulled out Ace's hard dick from his RockStar jeans and then she slid down her leggings before climbing on top of Ace and straddling his lap. She reached in between his legs and guided his big dick inside her slippery snatch. Palming her ass, Ace slammed Red up and down on his dick, she tossed her head back and took the dick as it hit her spot. Ace enjoyed how wet Red's pussy was. He'd heard from a few niggas around the hood that she had a wet-shot, and this turned out to be true, although it had a bit of a stench.

"Mmm... boy, this dick... feels so damn good!" Red panted in pleasure. She thrust her hips, allowing Ace's dick to go deep in her slit. Her moans grew louder as her cum oozed on Ace's dick and balls.

Once Ace felt himself about to bust a nut he lifted Red up off his dick and then she lowered her mouth onto it, sucking its tip and stroking its base in her hand. Ace rested his head back against the headrest and palmed Red's skull, guiding her mouth up and down on his erect cock. She flicked her tongue over the tip of his hardness and then licked her way down to his sac and back up before deep-throating it. He was in a trance, enjoying the feel of her oral pleasure.

"Damn shorty, your head game valid!" Ace complimented her. His toes curled as he reached climax and bust a nut in Red's mouth. Afterwards, he sent Red on her way.

As Ace dipped the Acura towards the crib he checked the time and saw it was now nearly eleven pm. Arriving at the apartment complex Ace parked beside Paris's Accord. He stepped out the car and tracked through the snow to the complex. Once inside the apartment, Ace kicked off his ACG Nike boots at the door and hung his Pelle Pelle coat on the rack. He found Paris and Adonis had fallen asleep on the couch in the front room with the flat screen TV on. As Ace turned off the TV, Paris stirred awake.

"Bae, I tried waiting up for you," Paris yawned.

"My fault. Somethin' came up," Ace deceived.

She stood and said, "Bring your black self on so we can go to bed."

"I'll be there after I take Adonis into his room." Ace scooped up his son into his arms and carried him to bed in his own bedroom. Then he made his way into the bathroom and quickly wiped his genitals clean. Once stepping into his and Paris's bedroom, Ace found Paris in bed snuggled beneath the covers. He unclothed down to his boxer-briefs and slid into bed alongside of his girl.

"Bae, I want you to cuddle with me till I fall asleep," Paris requested.

"I got you, boo." Ace spooned Paris and gave her a kiss on the neck. Before he knew it, they were both fast asleep.

•••

The next morning Ace was awakened by the sound of his iPhone buzzing on the nightstand. Morning light seeped into the bedroom through cracks of the window blinds and Ace covered his eyes from the brightness. He rolled over and noticed Paris was no longer in bed as he reached and grabbed the phone. Without checking the phone's display, he answered.

"Been hittin' you up for the past hour. Meet me at the trap so we go see Shane. And bring your re-up money with," said Chedda.

"A'ight. I'ma be there in a minute." Ace replied before ending the call. He yawned and stretched.

While Ace was talking on the phone Paris had entered the room. "Dude, don't tell me your ass already about to leave."

"Paris, I got some shit to tend to." Ace rolled out of bed.

"You always got something to tend to in the streets. Barely ever are you home. You really need to start spending more time with me and your son, Ace," she complained, standing in front of Ace with her arms folded and weight shifted to one side. And Ace knew she had every reason to complain, being that he ran the streets more than he was at home.

"Listen, Paris. I ain't got time for this shit..." Ace's words trailed off when he noticed Adonis standing near the doorway with a bowl of Froot Loops in hand.

"Later." Paris gave Ace a look that said their discussion wasn't over before ushering Adonis back towards the kitchen.

Making his way to the bathroom, Ace lifted the toilet seat to take a piss. He yelped in pain because as he pissed there was a burning sensation from his dick and he was well aware that he'd been burned with an STD after raw-doggin' Red. *I'ma fuck that hoe up*, he contemplated, seething. He couldn't have Paris finding out about him burning or she would never let him hear the end of it, so he'd have go and get it taken care of immediately. Luckily Paris didn't want some dick last night, he thought.

Ace took care of his whole nine before returning to the bedroom. He tossed on a black thermal, a pair of blue distressed Balmain jeans and black Balmain Taiga boots. Afterwards, he removed the very bottom drawer from the dresser where he stashed away his guns, drugs, and cash from Paris, only because he felt it was better she didn't know. He grabbed some cash and counted out his re-up and then pocketed it, before replacing the drawer and heading out the bedroom. He came upon Paris and Adonis seated on the couch in the front room watching TV, and once he went to give her a kiss she turned her head, offering him her cheek.

"Just go, Ace," Paris told him.

"It's like that, bae?" Ace said, detecting her attitude. Stepping to the front door, he grabbed his Pelle Pelle coat from the rack and slid into it, feeling the Glock inside the pocket. He bounced.

The streets were cleared of snow allowing Ace to rocket the Acura towards the hood. Arriving at the trap house, he slid the whip towards the curb and parked behind Chedda's

Audi. He stepped out the whip and headed inside the trap where he came upon Chedda seated on the couch and counting up his portion of the re-up money.

"Damn dawg, you ain't ready to ride yet?" Ace said as he took a seat beside his boy.

"Gotta make sure the bread right. Bring your half?" Chedda responded.

Ace pulled out his half of the paper and tossed it on the coffee table. "It's all there."

"No doubt." Chedda counted up all the re-up money to make absolutely sure it wasn't short a dollar. He always liked going to the plug with his money right. Having to re-up, Ace and Chedda was finna go see Shane to cop two bricks, and as usual Shane, would match what they'd cop and give it to them on consignment. It wasn't a problem for Ace and Chedda getting rid of the product, being that they had some niggas pushing packs and others they fronted weight. For the most part, they flooded the hood.

As Ace and Chedda slid through traffic in Chedda's Audi, they were on their way towards the south side of town to see Shane.

"You and Gee left a nigga hangin' last night so I had to make a couple bands by my lonely," Ace said.

"So, what'd you get into last night?" Chedda asked.

"Got into some burnin' pussy, that's what," Ace replied, seething.

Chedda glanced over at him with a quirked brow. "What you mean?"

"I fucked the hoe Red last night, and she burned a nigga." Ace shook his damn head and Chedda bust out laughing. "Dawg, that shit ain't funny. I gotta go and get this shit taken care of ASAP before my girl find out."

"Yeah, it is funny. Ace, you know Red's a thot, and you still smashed her raw. If Paris finds out you burnin', she gon' cut off your lil dick," Chedda chuckled.

All Ace could find fit to say was, "I'ma fuck Red up whenever I catch her hoe-ass."

Chedda pulled to the curb in front of the liquor store in the hood. While Chedda remained in the whip, Ace stepped inside and purchased a blunt and bottle of Hennessy. As Ace emerged from the store, he peeped the red Chrysler 300C pull to a stop behind the Audi. Stone stepped out of the Chrysler. Ace and Stone locked eyes as they crossed paths.

"Heard you back in the streets gettin' it in," Stone said.

"Apparently the streets are talkin'," Ace replied.

"Shorty, just stay out my way in these streets unless you want war." Stone's tone was assertive.

Ace scoffed. "I'ont mind bein' in the streets warrin' with killas."

The two glared at each other a moment before they went on their way. Ace saw Star was seated in the passenger side of the Chrysler and she looked away, not able to look Ace in his eyes. He figured she felt guilty for getting with his opp, of all niggas. Star had gotten with Stone and he wifed her up, they now lived together and even had a two-year-old daughter together. Still, Ace didn't take their relationship serious.

"Fuck was that about with Stone?" Chedda wanted to know as he started the whip.

"Nigga talkin' like he want war with us. Should air his ass out right now," Ace told him heatedly while gripping the Glock in his lap.

"Leave his ass be for now. He'll give us a reason for all-out war." Chedda pulled off into traffic. While riding shotgun Ace rolled up a blunt of green. The two bobbed their heads to sounds of Fredo Bang's "Dangerous" thumping from the speakers as they headed towards their destination. Yielding at a stop sign on 10th and Ring Street, Chedda checked the rearview mirror more so out of habit and noticed the Intrepid had been tailing them, while Ace was oblivious to it. And Chedda knew who was riding in the Intrepid.

"Mu'fuckas tailin' us," Chedda informed.

"You sure?" Ace peeped at the Intrepid through the rearview mirror and thought it looked familiar.

"Fa sho. Been on us for a few blocks now."

Ace gripped the pole in his lap and directed, "Let's air 'em out."

"Say no more." Chedda reached beneath his seat and came up with his Glock .19 with a thirty-shot clip.

The two jumped out the Audi simultaneously and aimed their poles at the Intrepid as it approached down the block. Once seeing Ace and Chedda with their guns aimed, the Intrepid immediately began to go into reverse but it wasn't fast enough.

Boc, boc, boc, boc!

Blocka, blocka, blocka!

Ace and Chedda sent slugs at the Intrepid hitting its front hood and windshield. They continued to fill the Intrepid with slugs until it backed its way off the block. Then hastily, Ace and Chedda jumped back into the Audi and sped off.

"Can't believe that nigga had the fuckin' audacity to try that," Chedda spat and slammed a fist onto the steering wheel.

"Fuck's that nigga?" Ace wanted to know while he watched the rearview mirror to be sure the Intrepid didn't reappear.

"It's that nigga Jay. His ass done fucked up." Once Chedda said the name, Ace then realized why the Intrepid looked so familiar.

"Then we gotta get down on his ass."

Chedda dipped around a vehicle in traffic and sped through a yellow light. "Don't trip. I'ma send a few lil niggas to spin on 'em."

Chapter 11

Ace puffed the blunt as he switched lanes in the Acura going up Fond du Lac Avenue. He rode by the Milwaukee Mall, which was infamous for its knockoff goods, and where no baller would be caught dead. He was on his way to the hood.

Ace happened to spot Quincy strolling hand-in-hand with a bitch through the mall's parking lot. He hadn't come across Quincy since his first day out when he had treated Quincy in the hood, and Ace was looking forward to addressing him about the idle threats Neesha had said Quincy made. Immediately, Ace bent into the lot where he braked to a stop behind Quincy's vehicle, barricading him in. Leaving the Acura idling, Ace jumped out and ran up on Quincy with his pole in hand. He stopped Quincy in his tracks as Quincy was finna step into his vehicle.

"Whussup, Q?" Ace accosted him assertively.

"N-n-nothin'..." Quincy stuttered as Ace stuck the barrel to Quincy's ribcage then frisked him and found no weapon.

"Neesha tells me you're talkin' 'bout I better watch my back and shit."

"Man, you know how Neesha ass is. She just mad I ain't fuckin' with her like that."

Ace eyed him sharply and warned, "Don't try me, Quincy." He returned to the Acura and sped off on his way.

Arriving at his destination, Ace pulled to the curbside in front of the trap spot that was run by his pusher, Marco. Ace texted him to come out. Marco made his way to the whip and stepped into the passenger seat. He was a dark-skinned, husky nigga with a Philly-fro and gold teeth. And Marco was a paper chaser.

"You got that paper?" Ace cut to the chase.

"Fa sho." Marco fished out a bankroll and then handed it over to him. As usual, Ace counted up the paper and it was all there. "Since I been frontin' you, the money never came up short. So I'ma front you more work than usual," Ace told him.

"I'm with that."

Ace handed Marco a four-and-a-split of soft white. "I'll be in touch."

"Do that," Marco replied. He then stepped out the whip and headed for the trap spot and Ace pulled off down the street.

In the hood, Ace posted on the block with Glen and some packboys as they were catching plays. Ace had graduated from having to post on the block, although he wouldn't forget those days and nights of being posted on the block with that pole cocked pushing his own packs.

Neesha and Red came making their way down the block on afoot, and Ace was still heated at Red's hoe-ass for burning him with gonorrhea. He'd been to the clinic to get it taken care of and was relieved that Paris hadn't let him fuck in a week, giving him time to clear up. Ace was looking forward to checking Red.

"Red, your hoe-ass burnt me! I'ont know why I even fucked you," Ace heatedly confronted her.

"What're you even talkin' 'bout, Ace?" Red feigned ignorance.

"Hoe, you the only one I fucked, so you know what I'm talkin' 'bout."

Red looked embarrassed. "I-I'm sorry, Ace."

"No, say sorry to my dick," he told her. In front of everyone Red knelt down and pulled his dick out his Balmain jeans and did as she was told. The packboys laughed aloud at the shit while Neesha shook her damn head.

"Ace, that shit ain't right," Neesha commented as she ushered Red away.

While posted up, Ace's line rang and he noticed the call was from a nigga he dealt with named Sonny Boy. He answered.

"Check it out, I need a book. Can you make that happen?" Sonny Boy asked.

"Fa sho. Just give me about an hour and I'll get back with you," Ace told him. He himself didn't have a kilo up for sale, yet he knew who he could middleman a deal through. After hanging up with Sonny Boy, Ace then dialed Phat.

"What it do, lil homie?" Phat answered.

"I need to get with you ASAP. It's some money in it for us both," Ace said.

"Sounds good 'cause money talks. Besides, I wanna put you up on a move anyway. Just meet me at my duck-off."

Hopping in the Acura, Ace headed to meet with Phat. During the commute he wondered what the hell move did Phat want to put him up on. Whatever it was, Ace was sure it would be lucrative because like himself, Phat was optimistic when it came to gettin' paid.

Arriving at the duck-off spot located out in the meadows, Ace parked out front behind Phat's silver Mercedes Benz G-wagon. Then he stepped out of the whip and approached the apartment and knocked on the front door. The door came open and he found the heavier Phat. Once Phat invited him inside, Ace peeped the two niggas in the front room, who were obviously Phat's shooters, Nice and Troy, counting up cash. It was apparent Phat had his money up judging by the numerous stacks of cash and the five bricks set out on the coffee table. While Phat led him into the kitchen, Ace admired the plush and lavishly furnished apartment.

"So, what's the deal?" Phat wanted to know.

"Got a nigga lookin' to cop a brick, and I need you to front me," Ace requested.

"Done. Now about the move I have on deck. So I got these cats comin' from outta town to cop some weight, and I want you to strip them and bring the work back to me."

"And what's in it for me?"

"Sixty G's. You in?"

Ace studied him a moment. "Yeah, I'm in."

"Then I'll give you the details when I come up with them," Phat told him. "Now, let's go and get you that brick."

•••

Ace stopped at the liquor store in the hood. He stepped outta his Acura and then entered the store where there were no other patrons inside. Once Ace approached the register, he greeted Abdul then requested two Swisher Sweets blunts and handed over a sawbuck. Abdul handed him the blunts and change along with a sack of budded weed.

"It's on me," Abdul said with a smirk on his lips. "There's more where that comes from."

"Fa sho."

After leaving the store Ace was headed to the crib. Paris had texted him earlier that she wanted for him to go out with her and Adonis tonight. Things between Ace and Paris were back cool after some makeup sex. Ace just wanted to keep his girl and son out of his street affairs. Arriving at the apartment complex, Ace parked and made his way inside and up to the apartment. He found Paris dressing their son when he walked into Adonis's bedroom.

"How long before you'll be ready to go?" Ace wanted to know.

Paris looked at him like something was the matter. "Dude, you ain't going nowhere with us looking like that. I already laid out an outfit for you in our bedroom for you to change into," she told him.

Ace took himself a quick shower and then changed into the red Nike jogger suit and a fresh pair of AirMax 95s that matched his girl and son's shoes. He set on the toilet and took a moment to roll up a blunt of the weed he received from Abdul, it was lime green and frosty. They took Paris's Accord on their way to Chuck E. Cheese, with Paris driving. During the commute they smoked on the blunt with all of the windows cracked an inch in order to air out the smoke so their son, who was in the back strapped into his car seat, wouldn't catch a contact high. Not even halfway through the blunt and they were high, and Ace thought he'd have to get with Abdul for more of the green. As they cruised along, Doja Cat's "Say So" played in the background.

"Mika keeps asking me when we'll get engaged and I tell her when the time's right," Paris was saying. She hit the blunt and then passed it to Ace. "Well, she says the right time was as soon as you came home from prison. I told her to just focus on her own relationship." Stopping at a stoplight, Paris glanced into the back to check on Adonis, who was quietly playing on his iPad. She then looked to Ace and asked, "Bae, you think we should get engaged soon?"

"We're already together and happy. Puttin' a ring on it won't make it better. Feel me?" Ace answered. He wasn't quite ready to commit himself to Paris solely because he was already committed to the game. Although he was aware that unlike the game, Paris would be loyal to him.

"You're right. All that matters is that we're together."

In the parking lot of Chuck E. Cheese, Paris found a parking spot. While she busied herself removing an excited

Adonis from his car seat, Ace discreetly placed his Glock beneath the passenger seat. He felt it wasn't a need to tote his pole inside the kid-friendly place. They headed inside.

While Paris occupied a booth awaiting their order of pizza to arrive, Ace took Adonis along with him to play some of the games. They were playing a racing car arcade game when Paris found them, she ushered them to the booth in order to eat the pizza. Ace and Adonis occupied one side of the booth while Paris sat across from them.

"Between you and your son, I don't know who's messier," Paris commented, seeing that both had gotten pizza sauce on their shirts.

"My son just be stuntin' like his daddy," Ace cracked and caused Paris to laugh.

"He definitely looks like you. And I'm sure he had to get being bad as hell from your genes. But of course he got being bright as hell from mine."

Ace grinned and replied, "I'ma let you have that." He took the last bite of his slice of pizza and then peered down at Adonis who picked a pepperoni from his shirt and stuffed it into his mouth.

"Ace?"

"Yeah?"

Paris hesitated before saying, "You know, I noticed what you put under the seat back in the car."

Ace wiped his mouth with a napkin. "It's just in case."

"In case what, Ace?" she pressed with concern rising in her voice.

"Look, Paris, don't act like you don't know. I ain't lettin' no nigga dishonor me or mine," he replied, trying to keep his cool.

Paris shook her head. "So that's all life's about for you is honor? Well, you don't have to be willing to die for honor

108

from niggas, Ace. Because you already have a family that honors you more than anyone," she responded sincerely.

"Real talk, you and Adonis are my life, Paris. And y'all gon' be that till the death of me."

"Then maybe you should cherish your 'life' more than you do." Paris's eyes grew misty with tears. "Look, I'm gonna take Adonis to play a while."

Ace chilled in the booth and thought on what was said while Paris had taken Adonis to go through the huge tunnel. He observed Paris while she stood watch over their son, and she just so happened to glance back over her shoulder at him catching his eyes, and then playfully stuck out her tongue at him. *Damn, she and my son mean so much to a nigga*, Ace contemplated.

During the ride home, Ace drove while a tired Paris rode in silence and Adonis was in back, strapped into his car seat and sound asleep. Ace found himself reflecting on the discussion he'd had with Paris, he knew what she was stressing was nothing but true because overall, he had her and his son to live for. Although in the streets it was death before dishonor.

•••

Ace had picked up Savvy and taken her out. The two had been getting to know each other via texts and FaceTime. And Ace took a liking to Savvy, he thought she was the type of bad bitch that was fit for a street nigga. But she wasn't wifey material, just a side-bitch. He had made her aware upfront that he was with Paris, although Savvy didn't seem to mind it.

Savvy on the other hand, was independent. At only twenty-six, Savvy had been around the block before so she was used to fuckin' with street niggas like Ace. She was a redbone, short with a slim-thick frame, rocked her hair long on one side while cut low on the other. Both her cheeks were pierced, among other places, and her skin was sprayed with tatts. And Savvy had an attitude problem but knew how to keep it cute.

Ace and Savvy were out at the hookah lounge. They were seated on the sofa where they conversed while having drinks and toking from a hookah. Ace just wanted to show Savvy a good time, being that it was their first time out together. And so far the night was going good.

"Boy, pass me the hookah," Savvy requested and Ace did so. She took a drag from the hookah and exhaled a thick cloud of smoke. Savvy noticed Ace admiring her. "What?" she said shyly.

"I'm just tryna figure out why a bitch as bad as you don't have a nigga in your life," Ace replied. He took a drag from the hookah.

"Well..." Savvy shifted uncomfortably in her seat. "I did have a nigga who I was with since we were teens until he passed a year ago. He was the daddy of my two kids, who now lives with their dad's mama," she expounded.

"If you don't mind, how'd he lose his life?"

Savvy took a breath. "He was shot to death when some niggas tried to rob him. And since then, I just decided to stay single until I meet the right nigga."

"And am I the right nigga?"

"Ace, I know how niggas like you are, because my baby daddy was the same way. You won't love a bitch more than you do the streets."

"Believe me, street niggas need love too." Ace smirked.

"And I'm sure your wifey loves you," she remarked.

"I'm sure she does too. But I get the vibe that you know how to love a street nigga the right way."

"Boy, please. You probably only want me for my pussy," she half-joked.

"I can get some pussy from any bitch. I like you for you, Savvy. And it's not just about your looks for me, what I like most about you is that you're down," he told her.

"Period!" Savvy concurred, knowing she was a down bitch.

Ace stopped a waitress as she came by. "Me and my girl would like a glass of Rémy," he ordered himself and Savvy drinks. He fished out his bankroll and peeled off a c-note then handed it to the waitress. "The rest is a tip."

The waitress went for their drinks and returned shortly. She set the glasses on the chaise positioned before Ace and Savvy and then went on her way. Ace grabbed up his drink and so did Savvy.

"I'd ask how you get to the bag, but it's apparent that you're a trapper," Savvy commented.

"And, what if I am a trapper?"

"Like I told you, my baby daddy was the same way so I don't have a problem with it. And hopefully, you don't have a problem with how I get my bag either."

"Listen boo, if you sell dope or start cookin', dancin' or sellin' pussy, it don't matter 'cause I'ont judge you," Ace assured her.

"Good to know. And just so you know, I'm a dancer," Savvy told him.

"And what's so wrong with that?"

"It seems most niggas don't take a bitch who strip like me serious. It's just a way to get a bag for me."

"Savvy, I ain't against bein' in a serious relationship with a dancer, if that's what you gettin' at."

"Then now I know." Savvy blushed.

Ace slipped a hand over Savvy's exposed tattooed thigh and said, "How 'bout some time I come to your club and see you perform?"

"I'm cool with that. Just be sure to bring lots of ones," Savvy half-joked. She sipped at her drink.

After having a good time at the hookah lounge, Ace was on his way to drop off Savvy. He pulled the Acura to the curb in front of her place and parked.

"Hopefully we can do this again soon," said Ace.

"The sooner the better." Savvy smiled. She stepped out the car and as she made her way up to the front door of her lower-level duplex home Ace admired her ass. He thought he'd be seeing more of her as he pulled off down the street.

Chapter 12

It had been nearly two weeks since Ace had fronted Marco the work and since then, he hadn't heard shit from Marco. So Ace decided to drop by Marco's trap spot. He lowered the volume on his music as he pulled the Acura to the curb before the trap where a few young thugs stood posted on the sidewalk. They strained to see through tinted windows and one clutched the pistol on his waist. Ace rode with his .9 Glock with the thirty on his lap so he wasn't worried about nothing. He dashed down the passenger window.

"That nigga Marco around?" Ace wanted to know.

The slimmer thug removed his hand from his pistol once recognizing Ace. "Haven't seen Marco in a few days," he informed.

Marco got me fucked up if his ass thinks he's just gonna run off on me, Ace contemplated as he pulled off.

In the hood, as Ace cruised up the block he beeped the horn at Reverend Johnson, who offered a wave while he was shoveling the snow on the sidewalk in front of his home. Around the corner, Ace parked in front of the trap spot and then departed the car and made his way into the trap. Upon entering, Beast-Mode excitedly jumped all over Ace until he pushed the dog away. In the front room, Ace found Chedda seated on the couch counting up profits from a flip, and Glen sat beside him weighing up product for a play. There was stacks of cash and ounces of coke and loaded pistols, all set out on the coffee table.

"Where you just come from?" Chedda asked without looking up from counting the paper.

"Lookin' for that nigga Marco. He ran off with some work I fronted him," Ace told him as he shrugged outta his Pelle Pelle jacket and tossed it over the arm of the couch.

"So, what you gon' do about him?"

"Chedda, you know ain't no nigga runnin' off without payback."

"Marco must not know we're the ones who do the bustin' moves on niggas," Glen added.

Ace pulled the pole off his waist and held it up. "Well, I'ma let Marco know when I catch his ass," he vowed. Ace set the pole on the coffee table. "Speakin' of, I got a move lined up."

"What's the move?" Chedda wanted to know, giving his undivided attention.

"A jack move. Phat got some marks comin' in from outta town to buy some keys, and he wants me to jack them," Ace laid it out.

"And what's the payout?"

"Sixty racks. You down?"

"Yeah, I'm down," Chedda agreed.

"And I'm down for whatever," Glen added.

Ace eyed both his boys. "I'll let y'all know when we'll move out."

•••

Ace and Chedda had been invited out by Shane. They settled in at a table near the back of the scene and popped some bottles. The two had hardly been together over the months, with Ace trying to establish himself in the game and Chedda trying to establish himself legitimately. Nonetheless, they were down for each other.

"Ace, you been trappin' hard since you got out, by now you should have some nice amount of G's stacked up," Chedda commented. "I mean, I ain't tryna count your

pockets, homie. But I'm curious what you're trappin' for."
He turned the bottle of Rémy up to his lips.

"I'm trappin' for me and mine. Gotta take care of my
girl and son. Feel me? Plus, watch the whip I pull out when
the summertime hit." Ace smirked.

Chedda shifted towards his boy. "I feel you on those
things, Ace, although there's more for us if we invest our
paper."

"Look Chedda, I'm down with whatever you thinkin'.
For now, I'ma just keep paper chasin'."

"Fa sho."

Shane approached the table. "Hope you niggas havin' a
good time. Yo Ace, shorty been eyein' you since you
stepped in this bitch." He pointed out a shorty who turned
out to be Tia and said, "How 'bout you go and see to her
while I rap with Chedda."

Tia was present with some of her homegirls. Throughout
the night a few niggas had approached her whom she turned
down. Ace had to admit she was earning the attention she
received by rocking a pair of black leather shorts that hugged
her hips and ass with a red jean jacket and fitted T-shirt both
leaving her navel ring exposed and a pair of red leather thigh
high stilettos. Shorty was dressed like a slut.

Bottle in hand, Ace approached Tia. "What're you doin'
here tonight?"

"What's it look like, just in here havin' some drinks with
my bitches," Tia replied with bit of a slur. She had a glass of
Henny in hand. Her homegirls eagerly wanted to know who
Ace was and Tia half-jokingly said to them, "He don't want
any of you hoes." She then gave her attention to Ace,
looking him up and down seductively. "Boy, I see you in
here lookin' all good and shit."

Ace figured she'd quaffed more liquor than she could handle so he ignored her comment and said, "Where's the kids, Tia?"

"Damn, nigga, they're at my mama's. Why you worried about all the wrong stuff right now?" She invaded Ace's personal space and pressed her breasts against him and Ace eased back.

"Shorty, you tipsy. You should go home for the night."

"Ace, I'm a grown-ass woman, so don't try telling me what to do." She copped an attitude.

"Look, you know Cain wouldn't want you out here like this."

"Cain don't love me like I love his ass! If he did then he wouldna left me and his kids out here by ourselves! So I'ont wanna hear shit about what Cain wants!" Tia vented.

"How 'bout you let me take you home."

Tia took a brief second to respond. "Okay. But lemme finish my drink real quick."

Ace left her to down her drink with her homegirls while he returned to the table where Chedda was rapping with Shane.

"Fam, I'm finna bounce," Ace informed.

Chedda peeped at his Rolex timepiece. "Already? It ain't even twelve yet."

"See you finna bounce with shorty." Shane smirked.

"It ain't even like that. Chedda, I'll get with you tomor-row," Ace said before he shook up with Chedda and stepped away to find a tipsy Tia.

During the ride, Ace sparked up a half-smoked blunt that was in the ashtray. As he pushed the Acura towards Tia's place, music played in the background. Summer Walker's "Girls Need Love" played into rotation.

"Oooh, this my song!" Tia exclaimed. She sang along off-key.

Ace shook his head and said, "Shorty, you need to stop."

"Boy, whatevs!"

Arriving at Tia's apartment Ace pulled to the curb. "Go inside and get yourself some sleep," he told her.

"Thought you'd come inside with me." Tia offered him a seductive look.

"Tia, take your ass inside and get some sleep."

"Stop frontin' like you don't wanna fuck me, Ace." Tia leaned in then kissed him and grabbed at his crotch. Instantly Ace removed her from him altogether.

"You know Cain my nigga, so you outta line, Tia, and you need to find your fuckin' place!" Ace checked her ass.

"Whatever, Ace! Fuck you!" Tia snapped. She threw open the passenger door, snatched up her purse, hurried out, and then slammed shut the door before she stormed off.

Cain had about three months until he'd get out of prison, and Ace planned to get money with Cain when he returned to the streets. He just hoped that Cain would realize how Tia was a no-good-ass hoe. And whenever he called, then Ace would be sure to let Cain know.

Ace skirted off, thinking, *These hoes ain't loyal.*

•••

Ace pulled the Acura to the curb on the block and parked. He stepped out the car and posted on the block with Glen and some packboys. The block was filled with hustle and bustle as droves of smokers came and went, coppin' rocks.

While taking a call, Ace leaned back up against the Acura. One of the packboys yelled out "Twelve!" then Glen and the others began to scatter as the unmarked Dodge Magnum sped down the block. But before Ace was able to flee himself, a plainclothes detective had hopped out the car and ran up on him, brandishing his service weapon.

"Freeze! Don't move!" the dick demanded. It was the dirty cop Lucas. He was a Hispanic guy with a slick back ponytail. And in the hood he was known to extort drug dealers, plant bogus evidence, rough up suspects, and anything else dirty he could get away with. Not to mention his partner, Detective Bradshaw, was the same.

"Man, what the fuck," Ace grumbled as Lucas handled him roughly and slammed him up against the car.

"Shut the hell up!" Lucas hit him with a solid blow to the ribs. He then gave Ace a frisk, just so happened he'd left his pole inside the car. Lucas pulled out a bankroll from Ace's pocket then stated, "I'm sure this is drug money, knowing you. Well, now it belongs to me."

"You can't just rip me off," Ace complained.

"How about I arrest you for drug loitering and anything else my partner finds around here instead," Lucas threatened as Bradshaw was searching the area, and Ace was sure he'd find something prohibited.

"You got it," Ace caved. He knew Lucas would keep using his badge as leverage if he wasn't dealt with.

"Thought so. I'd gotten word you were back out, Ace. And word is you're back to your old ways," Lucas said derisively.

Ace scoffed. "And I see you're still up to your old ways."

"Don't think I'll let you get away with a damn thing." Lucas jabbed a finger into his chest with each word.

Bradshaw stepped up after confiscating some sacks and a pistol and asked, "Whose is this, Ace?"

"I got a right to remain silent," Ace replied.

"Don't even bother, Bradshaw. He won't snitch," Lucas told his partner. "Ace, you may not get so damn lucky next time around." He and Bradshaw hopped into their unmarked Magnum and dispelled down the block.

Once Twelve left, Glen and the others came back. He said, "I hope those boys didn't find my sack."

•••

"There the niggas go now." Ace pointed out the marks as they headed for the Yukon Denali. He, along with Chedda, Glen, and a hitter from around the hood, Lil D, were all strapped while they sat parked in a trapper car across the street from the seedy Diamond Inn Hotel. Ace rolled shotgun while Chedda and Glen took up the backseat, and Lil D was the designated driver. The gang observed the three marks step inside the Denali, one carrying a tote bag. These were the marks from outta town that Phat had put Ace up on. The marks had just come from making a drug deal with Phat, and now they were on their way back to Minnesota. But not before they would be robbed.

The Denali's headlights beamed in the night as it made its way out of the parking lot and submerged into traffic. Tailing the Denali, Ace n'em blended in with traffic so not to be made by the marks before they had the chance to bust them down. The Denali yielded to a stop at the stoplight while positioned betwixt vehicles before and behind it. Once Lil D pulled up beside the Denali, the others jumped out the trapper brandishing guns. Ace hurried to the driver's door, Glen the back door and Chedda went around to the passenger door, they caught the marks off guard.

Ace ripped open the door then pressed his Draco to the driver's neck and immediately grabbed the FN handgun out of his lap, stuffing it on his own waist. Glen invaded the backseat and then used his Glock .26 with a thirty-shot clip to slap the nigga in the backseat across the face, splitting his brow. Chedda had smashed out the passenger side window with the butt of his MAC .11 and leveled on the passenger's face. They were ready to murk the marks if they had to.

"I dare you niggas to try somethin'," Ace threatened through clenched teeth.

"Where the mu'fuckin work and shit at?" Chedda demanded to know.

"R-right here," the nigga in the backseat stammered as blood trekked down his face.

Glen pressed the Glock to his dome. "Run that shit, nigga!"

"A'ight, a'ight!" the nigga said pleadingly. He reached beside himself and grabbed the tote bag, then handed it over to Glen, who peeped inside to make sure it was the product. The nigga in the backseat went to draw a pistol on Glen and then Ace turned aim on the nigga and let off.

Boc, boc, boc!

The nigga in the backseat took slugs in his face and chest, his body slumped on its side lifeless. Ace brandished the Draco around the interior of the vehicle menacingly and the terrified driver and passenger threw their hands up in surrender. After confiscating the product, Ace n'em hurried back into the trapper and Lil D peeled off down the street through the stoplight and nearly caused a collision. As planned, they returned to the hotel where Phat remained. Pulling into the parking lot, they parked beside Phat's G-wagon. Ace grabbed the blood spattered tote bag then stepped outta the trapper with the Draco strapped around his shoulder on full display, then he stepped into the G-wagon.

He and Phat took up the backseat while Nice and Troy stood outside on security.

"Everything good, lil homie?" Phat inquired. Ace set the tote bag on the seat betwixt them. Grabbing the bag by its strap, Phat held it up and snorted, "Blood on the dope."

"Sometimes a nigga gotta get paid in blood." Ace smirked.

"It all spends just the same." Phat unzipped the bag and then checked the product finding the expected four bricks inside, all wrapped in cellophane. "It's all here."

"Fa sho. Now let me get me," Ace replied.

Phat dug into a brown paper bag and came out with the pay from the cash the marks had just spent with him for the work. He handed some stacks over to Ace and said, "That's 60 G's. There's more where this comes from, Ace."

"More money, more problems. But I ain't worried about nothin'," Ace told him and patted the Draco. They shook up before Ace stepped outta the G-wagon and then stepped into the passenger seat of the trapper.

During the ride towards the hood, Ace n'em smoked on a blunt of loud while listening to Tee Grizzley's "Sweet Thangs."

"We have to get rid of the trapper, being that Twelve may be lookin' for it," Ace said. "Lil D, pull into the alleyway."

As directed, Lil D turned into the dim lit alley and pulled over. Right then, to Lil D's dismay, Glen stuck the Glock to the back of his dome.

Blam!

Lil D's blood and brain matter splattered all over the front windshield and his corpse slumped over the steering wheel. Ace had never planned to break bread with Lil D, and Chedda and Glen was in on it. While Ace stood on lookout,

Chedda and Glen removed the body from the car then stuffed it inside its trunk. The trio then headed off afoot, leaving Lil D's body unceremoniously dumped in the trunk.

Chapter 13

Since Ace had returned home a few months came and went. Although it seemed the only thing he kept track of was his profits and product. Alone at the crib, Ace pulled out his entire stash and did inventory. He'd counted up sixty-some G's and was working with five pounds of loud and a brick of yae. Not to mention, he'd added a Draco and an FN handgun, along with a Kevlar bulletproof vest to his arsenal. Ace wasn't exactly where he wanted to be in the game, however he was fast on the come-up.

Paris entered the apartment carrying a sleep Adonis. She took Adonis into his room and laid him in his bed. Then she made her way into her and Ace's bedroom where she found Ace looking over his stash. Although Paris was aware that Ace was trappin', she wasn't aware of his stash spot in their home. Ace figured it was for her own good, therefore she'd remain unattached to his street affairs.

"Ace, I told you not to have any of that shit around me and your son," Paris griped.

"Why you trippin' on me, and I'm out in the streets dodgin' cases and bullets to take care of us?" Ace stressed.

"Because not only are you putting yourself in harm's way, you're putting me and your son in harm's way also."

"Listen, you don't have to worry about that because I ain't."

"Maybe you should be worried." She stood with her arms folded and her weight shifted to one side.

Ace jumped to his feet and sniped, "How 'bout I just take my shit and go." He grabbed up a Nike gym bag from the closet and began packing his stash inside.

"Where are you going, Ace?" Paris insisted to know.

Ace just ignored her as he finished packing up his stash. He then stormed out the apartment with the bag in hand. Outside, he jumped into his Acura and tossed the bag into the passenger seat. Then he skirted off down the street. Ace was heated behind the issue with Paris back at the crib. But looking it from her side, he supposed it wouldn't have been much of an issue had he made her aware of the stash spot. And he was sure her issue wasn't about the cash being there as much as it was about the drugs and guns. Now she wouldn't have to worry about his stash being there at all.

Once Ace pulled to a stop at a stoplight he grabbed his iPhone and dialed Savvy. She answered.

"Where your ass at?" Ace wanted to know.

"Home. Why, what's up with you?" Savvy asked curiously.

"I'll let you know when I get there," he told her as he pulled off with traffic once the light flipped green.

Arriving at Savvy's place, Ace parked behind her Chrysler Sebring. He grabbed the bag from the passenger seat then stepped out the Acura and made his way towards the duplex home. Savvy stood at the door in a fitted baby T-shirt and leggings awaiting him. They hugged before he entered and she locked the door then led him inside the front room. Savvy had company over, seated on the couch, it was her younger brother, Dre, and her bestie, Nina.

"I need to talk with Sav alone so you two gotta go," Ace insisted.

"Come again?" Nina responded.

"Nigga, don't come in here like you runnin' shit," Dre remarked and hurried onto his feet.

"What, nigga?" Ace mugged him.

Savvy piped in. "Look, Dre, just go so I can talk with him. I'll get with you two tomorrow."

Dre looked to Savvy. "But, sis—"

"I said that I'll get with you tomorrow Dre," Savvy iterated, cutting him off. "Now would you please go? And Nina, I'll call you."

Nina grabbed her handbag then hugged her bestie before heading for the door, and Dre mugged Ace as he trailed her. Once alone with Savvy, Ace removed the FN from his waist and set it, along with the bag, on top of the coffee table before he flopped down on the brown leather couch. Savvy took a seat beside him folding her legs beneath her.

"So, Ace, what's up with you now?" Savvy pried.

"It's wifey. She's trippin' on a nigga and shit," Ace breathed.

"Mm. Sounds like we both gonna need a drink for this one." Savvy stepped over to the small cabinet and grabbed a partially full bottle of Rémy then returned to her seat in the couch. She sipped from the bottle before passing it to Ace. "Now, what about wifey?"

"Her ass trippin' on me over nothin'." Ace turned the bottle up to his lips and gulped down the liquor.

"Maybe she got a valid reason to trip."

Ace glanced over at her. "So, now you're on her side?"

"I'm just keepin' it real. Because after dealing with so many niggas I've learned that a lot of times y'all just don't get it. So, what is she trippin' over?"

"She have an issue with me keepin' my stash and shit at the crib around her and my son. So I packed my shit up and bounced," he explained.

"So she does have a valid reason," Savvy told him. "And you shouldn't have just walked out on her like that. But fortunately, you have me to come to," she added curtly.

"I just wanted to get my stash out the crib."

"Is that what's in the bag?"

"Yeah." Ace unzipped the bag, allowing her to see the contents herself. "And I need to stash it at your place for now." He grasped her by the nape of the neck then grabbed up his FN and brandished the gun in her face and forewarned, "Bitch, if you run off with my shit, then I'ma find you and body your ass."

"Ace, I ain't gonna run off with your shit. Don't even come at a bitch like that," Savvy remarked. She stood. "Come with me. And bring your bag." Savvy headed into her bedroom with Ace following. She went over to the closet which favored a miniature boutique with all of her designer heels, clothes, and handbags neatly stored away. Then she opened the hidden compartment beneath the floorboard where she had numerous stacks of cash and a baby Glock .9 of her own stashed away. "You can stash your things here with mine. It's a spot my baby daddy used when he was alive. And since your things will be here, I'll give you a key to my place."

"Sounds good." Ace felt comfortable with stashing his possessions there because he figured since Savvy was willing to give him a key to her place, then no other nigga had access to rip him off. He stashed his things away.

Savvy walked up on him and said, "If don't no bitch got you, I got you."

She wrapped her arms around the nape of his neck and he held her close at the waist while they kissed. Ace's phone began to ring and he checked its display, seeing it was Paris. He pressed "ignore" then set the phone on the nightstand before returning his undivided attention to Savvy. She pushed him back onto the bed then knelt and pulled out his dick from his Balmain jeans and began toppin' him off. Savvy flicked her pierced tongue over the tip of Ace's enlarged dick then slowly took it in its entirety down her throat to the balls. He palmed the back of her skull and guided her mouth up and down on his hardness.

"Aah, shit boo. You suckin' me like a savage," Ace groaned.

"Mmmm... You like that?" Savvy purred, looking up into his eyes.

"Hell yeah... you doin' that." After a while Ace felt a nut swell up in the tip of his dick and he busted in her pretty mouth.

Savvy climbed onto her feet and pulled her shirt off over her head then her bra, revealing her erect, pierced nipples. She slid down her leggings and stepped out of them, and while standing there ass naked, Ace admired her tattooed and curvy body. Then she assisted him out of his Balmain sweatshirt, tossing it on the floor with her own garments followed by doing the same with his jeans. She straddled his lap while he sucked and licked on her nipples as he slid two fingers inside her wetness, causing her to let out soft moans.

"Mmm... oh, yes," Savvy moaned as she bucked up and down on his fingers like a dick.

"Damn, boo. A nigga feel how wet this pussy is." Ace finger-fucked her, making her pussy wetter.

"Oooh... Stop teasing me, nigga... Fuck me!" Savvy grabbed his dick and guided it deep inside her wet-wet. Ace gripped all that ass on her in both hands while she slammed herself up and down on the dick. "Oh, fuck... this dick so big... it got a bitch goin'." She tip-drilled his dick, repeatedly bringing her pussy up to its tip and back down to the base.

"Yeah, boo, ride this dick just like that," Ace encouraged. He held her by the hips and met her motions as he thrust his dick all up in her slit.

"Oooh shit, boy... I'm cuuummmin'!" Her warm juices oozed all over him.

"Yeah, cum all over this dick."

Before Savvy knew it, Ace rolled her onto her back, he got in between her legs and slipped his hardness inside of her. As Ace long stroked her, he sucked and licked on her nipples. She spread her legs, giving him more room to dig deeper into her as her back arched off the bed. It seemed the deeper his dick went, the wetter her pussy became.

"Turn around so a nigga can beat this pussy up from the back," Ace demanded her. Savvy turned and positioned herself on all fours and arched her back, then Ace filled her pussy with his dick.

"Fuck this pussy, Ace. Fuck it good!"

"A'ight, bitch." Ace fucked her from behind while smacking her ass, and she threw the pussy back on him.

"Oh, shit... this dick so big..." Savvy cried out. She stuffed her face into the pillow and took the dick.

"That's right, boo. Take this dick for me."

"Oooh... mmmm... yaaasss!" Savvy moaned loudly. She came again, her cum ran down Ace's inner thighs. He enjoyed the feel of her wetness surrounding his dick and he hit the pussy deeper. Savvy began throwing the pussy back harder.

"Damn, shorty... This pussy got a nigga about to bust a nut!"

"Bust that nut for me, boy," Savvy purred while looking back at it. After several more strokes Ace pulled himself out of her and then jerked his dick. "Yaaas... Nigga, lemme feel that warm nut all on my ass," she cooed. Ace bust his warm, gooey nut on her ass and lower back. She pulled him to her and kissed him greedily.

After fuckin' they lay in bed. Ace ran his fingers through her hair while Savvy rested her head on his chest. Ace didn't know if it was the pussy that had him thrown, but he felt that Savvy wanted to be more to him. And Savvy liked being with Ace, although she understood her position with him.

"Damn Sav, you almost got a nigga wanna make you wifey," Ace half-joked, running his hand over the curves of her body.

Savvy peered at him. "And maybe I wouldn't have a problem with it if you didn't already have a wifey," she told him.

"But you the type of bitch a nigga need by his side."

"And what type of bitch is that?"

"You know, a ride or die bitch," Ace told her.

Savvy smirked, like she knew she that ride or die. "And what type of nigga are you, Ace?" she asked.

"I'm just me, boo."

"And that's why a bitch feels some type of way about you."

Savvy shifted her body and took Ace's dick back into her mouth until it rocked up again, slobbered all over it, sucked his balls, then climbed back on top of him. She slid down on his dick and rode it.

•••

Savvy shook Ace awake. "Nigga, get your ass up and answer your damn phone. It's more than likely your wifey blowin' you up, like she's crazy," she said with resentment in her tone.

Ace grunted as he rolled over facing her. *The bitch probably already checked to see who's callin'*, he contemplated. After yawning and stretching, he reached over Savvy and grabbed his phone off the nightstand then noticed the caller was none other than Paris. *Lemme talk to her ass real quick,* he thought.

"S'up," Ace answered. He sat up on edge of the bed.

"Ace, why haven't you been answering your phone?" Paris said, sounding more relieved to hear from him than upset.

"A nigga just needed a moment to clear my head. So I stayed at the trap in the hood," Ace deceived her.

Savvy found her way into Ace's lap then kissed his neck and nibbled his earlobe. She whispered into his ear, "I want this dick so bad. Meet me in the shower when you're done with wifey." Climbing out of his lap, she strutted her nakedness into the bathroom, leaving him with a hard-on.

"I just want you to come home, Ace," Paris said, pleading.

"Listen, I'll be home soon. We'll talk then."

After ending his call, Ace centered the steamy bathroom and stepped into the shower. He found Savvy caressing her pussy. Bending her over, he slid his hardness inside her slit from behind and fucked her good.

It was afternoon when Ace headed for the hood in his Acura. He was on his way to check on how things was going with the latest re-up. Normally, it didn't take long for the work to be flipped with Ace and Chedda having a few trap spots around the city. But the trap spot in the hood was where they distributed most of the weight.

Arriving at the trap, Ace parked behind Chedda's Audi. As Ace stepped out the Acura, Chedda emerged from the trap.

"What's up, my G?" Ace asked.

"On my way to serve the nigga Rex," Chedda told him. "Look, I got a boss move that I wanna discuss with you. But it'll have to wait until later on."

130

"A'ight. Catch you later."

Ace made his way towards the trap as Chedda stepped into his whip. Inside the trap, Ace came upon Glen and his two homeboys, Poppa and Bookie, all counting up cash and bagging up work. He liked having the trio around because they were young savage niggas. Glen had been homeboys with Poppa and Bookie since the sandbox. Poppa was brown-skinned, slim with a nappy fro and he was more of a shooter, and Bookie was light-skinned, short with waves and was more of a trapper. Both were down for whatever.

"How that count lookin'?" Ace asked as he stepped up on Glen, who was counting up profits at the kitchen table.

"Just counted up twenty G's. And still got more to go," Glen told him.

"And how much work left?"

"Over a half-brick," Bookie answered. He weighed up eighths on the scale.

"But it'll all be gone by tomorrow," Poppa added as he bagged up the work.

"A'ight. Just make sure the profits come back right," Ace told them.

"Say no more," Glen replied.

"Check it out, I gotta get dip. I'll be back later," Ace said.

Glen stood. "Need you to give me a ride. Poppa and Bookie can finish up here."

"No problem. I'll be waitin' out in the car."

While awaiting Glen, Ace sat in the Acura and rolled up a blunt. It wasn't as cold in the car being that the weather was warming up and snow was melting as the springtime crawled close. Ace sparked the blunt while he thought about how he missed out on three consecutive summers when he was on lock, and he intended to pull out when the summer-time hit.

Ace's thoughts were interrupted when someone tapped on the passenger window. He saw it was a nigga from around the hood named Skinny, who was a two-timing hustler. He didn't much fuck with Skinny because the nigga was known to run his mouth too fuckin' much. Ace only cracked open the window.

"Skinny, what're you doin' creepin' on me? Damn near got popped doin' that shit," Ace told him, gripping the FN lying across his lap.

"I ain't the nigga you need to be worried about tryna creep on you out here," Skinny replied.

"What do you mean by that?" Ace puffed the blunt.

"Heard that nigga Stone been talkin' 'bout since you and Chedda not coppin' weight from him, then he's gonna shut y'all down. But you ain't hear that from me."

"Don't trip, I'll keep that between us."

"Anyway. I came by to cop an eight-ball," Skinny requested. Ace pulled out a sack and exchanged the dope for the cash. Skinny examined the product and said, "This dope looks like straight drop!"

Ace puffed the blunt. "You get what you pay for."

Glen made his way to the car and shouldered Skinny then stepped into the passenger seat. He didn't like Skinny at all because the nigga always ran his mouth. Ace passed Glen the blunt then he puffed it and blew smoke in Skinny's face. Leaving Skinny fanning smoke away, Ace pulled off down the street with he and Glen laughing.

"Fuck that nigga Skinny was talkin' 'bout?" Glen asked, knowing how Skinny talked too much.

"Claims he heard Stone been talkin' 'bout shuttin' us down," Ace told him.

"Dawg, who the fuck Stone think he is? Been waitin' for a while to spin on him." Glen was aware that Ace and Stone were beefin'. Ace's crew had been shooting it out with Stone's crew over control of the hood, and bodies had dropped on either side.

"Just be patient, we'll spin on Stone's ass," Ace assured. "Until then, we'll get to the bag."

On the way to drop off Glen, Ace took him to McDonald's as he requested in order to grab a bite to eat for Kiki. Glen had been fuckin' with Kiki for a few months, and the two really were into each other. It was funny to Ace how Glen and Kiki always argued one day and then the next day it was like nothing happened. Glen wouldn't admit it but Ace could tell that he loved Kiki. With a caramel complexion, long braids, and a curvy frame, Kiki was a pretty girl. And unlike her hoe-ass sister Red, Kiki kept her pussy on reserve.

Coming upon McDonald's Ace bent the Acura into the parking lot and found a parking spot. Before they could step out the whip, Ace's phone rang. Checking its display, he saw the caller was Phat. While Ace took the call, Glen went inside the fast-food joint.

"What's to it?" Ace said.

"Need to get up with you. Got a move for you," Phat told him.

"A'ight. Where you wanna meet up at?"

"Stop by the bitch Queen's spot later on. I'll be there."

"Bet," Ace replied before the two hung up. That gave him time to take his ass home to Paris and straighten things out with her before going to Queen's spot.

Glen returned to the car and Ace proceeded on his way to drop him off. Pulling up in front of Kiki's crib, Ace braked the Acura in the middle of the street. He and Glen shook up before Glen stepped out with the bag of food. He made his way towards the duplex house where Kiki was standing on the porch awaiting him, and she waved at Ace who chopped her the deuces.

At a glance Ace noticed Red seated in the passenger side of some nigga's car which was parked at the curb. Ace had been waiting to catch the hoe since he had been told by Neesha and some others that Red claimed she was pregnant by either himself or another nigga. He did fuck her without a condom, although he was absolutely sure to make the hoe swallow his seeds. So he wasn't having her put a baby on him.

I'm about to check this hoe, Ace thought, seething. Before stepping out the car he placed its gear in park and then hopped out with the car idling and leaving the driver's door wide open. He approached the passenger side of the car Red occupied and ripped the door open on her, and she looked at him dumbfounded.

"Hoe, stop goin' around claimin' you pregnant by me," Ace demanded.

"What do you mean, Ace, you know we fucked," Red replied.

"And I regret that we did. But you know I nutted in your mouth, so stop with the bogus-ass claims."

The nigga whose car it was jumped out and over the rooftop, he said, "Nigga, what's your damn problem? Back up off my ride before—" His words were cut once Ace drew the FN from his waist and slammed it down on the rooftop with a thud as a warning. "You got it," the nigga backed down and with no further words, he sat his ass back in the car.

"Red," Ace began, "like I said, stop claimin' I got your thot-ass pregnant 'cause we both know it isn't true." He turned for his whip and noticed Glen and Kiki both still standing on the porch watching the entire episode. Glen chuckled while Kiki just shook her head as Ace stepped inside the Acura and then stabbed off.

Pulling into the apartment complex's parking lot, Ace parked beside Paris's Accord. Before stepping out he placed the FN beneath the seat. He entered the building and made his way to the apartment, and when he stepped inside he found Paris and Adonis seated on the couch watching TV. Adonis jumped off the couch and hurried over to his daddy, and Ace embraced his son before Adonis went back to the couch. Then Paris stepped up to Ace and he grabbed her at the waist and she wrapped her arms around the nape of his neck.

"Don't think I still ain't mad at you for just leaving like that last night. And lemme find out your ass went and laid up with another bitch," Paris half-joked.

"I know I shouldna just bounced on you. My bad. And I realize why you don't want me to have that kind of shit around you and my son," Ace told her.

"Then where are you gon' keep it, if not here?"

"Don't even worry about it, Paris. I got it taken care of. All I need you to worry about is takin' care of home."

"And I will." She stood on her tiptoes and pecked his lips. "Bae, I think you need a hot shower and some food."

"Sounds good."

Ace made his way into the bedroom while Paris went into the kitchen. He got his things together and then took himself a shower. Once stepped out the shower, he noticed there was a text message on his phone from Savvy. While Paris was still in the kitchen cooking, he read the text.

SAVVY:
Wifey expect a nigga at home tonight?

Ace replied with a text.

ACE:
Yeah. But I'm sure you'll find another nigga
to take my place.

SAVVY:
Ace, miss me with that. Have a nice time thinking
about me while you're with wifey. LBS ;-)

ACE:
You so damn full of yourself. SMH.

SAVVY:
True... I gotta get ready for work. TTYL.

While Ace was dressing himself, he decided to phone
Chedda. He figured since Chedda wanted to rap with him
then they could get that chance later tonight.
"S'up, my G?" Chedda answered.
"I'm stoppin' by Queen's spot tonight. You should come
with me," Ace suggested.
"Cool. I can come."
"First come through and scoop me up in about an hour,"
Ace instructed before they ended the call.
Making his way into the kitchen Ace came upon Paris
making him a plate of mac & cheese and fried chicken. He
sat at the table with his girl and son and ate as a family. Once
he was done eating, Ace let Paris know he'd be stepping out
for a while and she told him to make sure he don't bring his
ass home too late. He knew she just wanted him home for the
night.

Once Chedda texted that he was outside, Ace left out. He went and grabbed his FN from beneath the seat in his car before stepping into Chedda's Audi. While they rolled through traffic headed for Queen's spot, Lil Poppa's "Dangerous" played at a modest volume. At the intersection on Sherman Boulevard and Capital Drive, Chedda turned left heading eastbound. It was beginning to grow dark out, so he flicked on the headlights. While they rolled along, Ace thought back on what he'd heard about Stone and decided to run it across Chedda.

"Get this, I heard the nigga Stone talkin' 'bout he's gonna shut us down since we ain't coppin' weight from him," Ace told him.

"Stone fuck around and get his ass burnt if he try some shit like that." Chedda scoffed.

"No cap."

Chedda pulled to a halt at a stop light. "My nigga, I been thinkin' about a boss move for us. We need to invest into somethin' legit."

"Somethin' legit like what?"

"Like a strip joint."

"You serious, huh?"

Chedda glanced at him and said, "As serious as an indictment. Listen, this move will be in our best interest because it'd be a front that'll keep the feds at bay. Most trap gods fail to invest into something legitimate in order to launder their dirty money. And that most likely leads to them doing Fed time. The only thing you'd need to do is invest your share and I'll take care of the rest. Of course it'll take some time and effort, although it'll be worth it."

Ace could tell that Chedda had thought it out. "I'm all for it whenever you're ready," he let Chedda know.

Arriving at Queen's spot, they parked nearby the house. Queen was a bitch who ran a gamble spot that most of the ballers throughout the Mil came to win or lose big money. Ace and Chedda knew that if it wasn't Queen's security, then there were no guns in the place, so they left their poles in the car while they entered the spot. The gamble spot reeked of weed. Niggas were in there making wagers on every game you could think of. And some bitches were sack-chasin', tryna come up on a baller. Typical shit.

Ace found Phat there taking part in a game of craps. "Glad you made it," he acknowledged Ace. He and Chedda also knew one another through Baller. "Why don't you get in on this gamble and we'll discuss that move afterwards."

During the dice game, they all placed bets. There was a young nigga named Pig who couldn't seem to lose on the dice, he'd won big and had several niggas eager to win back their cash, including Phat. Pig stepped away going to take a bathroom break. And after a while, when someone went to fetch him, they'd discovered he had vanished with the winnings, having jumped out the bathroom window. Pig had won upwards to eighty G's, and he knew he wasn't guaranteed to walk outta the spot without being robbed and possibly bodied for the paper. Now he would have niggas gunning for him for running off.

After leaving the gamble spot Phat had decided to give Ace a ride being that he wanted to talk with him, so Chedda went on his way. Phat and Ace were in the backseat of the G-wagon and Phat's two boys rode up front, Nice drove while Troy took up shotgun.

"Shit, I can't believe I got hit for that much paper," Phat griped. "It's nothin' to get right back. Anyway, I wanna rap with you about a trip I'm gonna take to Chicago to make a big drug deal, and I'll need another gun along that I can trust. And judgin' by the last move, you won't mind puttin' in gun-work if needed."

"What's in it for me?"

"Ten G's. You down?"

"I'm down for whatever," Ace took him up on his offer.

"I'll let you know when we'll make the trip, just have your gun locked and loaded," Phat told him.

Shortly thereafter, they pulled up in front of Ace's place. He shook up with Phat before stepping out the whip and then heading inside the complex. It was sometime after eleven pm when he got in into the crib, and it was quiet. Ace checked in on his son who was sound asleep in his bedroom. He then made his way into his and Paris's bedroom, where he found her sleeping only in one of his tank tops. After undressing down to his boxer-briefs, Ace slid into bed beside Paris and she snuggled back against him.

Undoubtedly, Ace loved Paris with his heart, although he had Savvy on his mind.

Martell "Troublesome" Bolden

Chapter 14

During the trip to Chicago, Ace and Phat along with his two boys checked into the Days Inn hotel. Nice and Troy carried the baggage inside which contained cash and artillery.

Once they were settled into their room, Phat ordered room service. Shortly thereafter, there was a knock on the door. Nice answered the door for the room service and tipped the bellhop, who brought two bottles of Dom P. on chill in a bucket of ice. Troy set on the couch rolling up a couple of blunts for them to smoke on. And Ace checked out the spread of the city from the window.

Phat stepped up beside Ace with a bottle in hand. "'Preciate you ridin' along with me and my boys. No matter how many times I make this trip, I still come strapped. A nigga can never be too safe when there's lots of cash and product at stake." He turned the bottle up to his lips.

"Better safe than sorry," Ace replied, knowing the chances of niggas scheming.

"Ace, all you'll need to do is keep your eyes on the money and your finger on the trigga. Nice and Troy already know this."

"Enough said."

"Listen up," Phat addressed all. "I won't be meetin' up with my plug until tomorrow. So since we have time to spare, I figure we could hit the town."

In the Lincoln Navigator rental the gang cruised through downtown Chi, making their way to the many outlets on Michigan Avenue. Ace stopped by several of the outlets, purchasing attire from Gucci, Prada, and Nike to name a few. He couldn't forget about Paris and Adonis, being sure to pick them up a few things. Also, he picked up something for Savvy. Ace had splurged and spent several G's. After the shopping spree, they stopped by the famous Black Ink tattoo shop. Ace decided to have "RICH $AVAGE" tatted across his chest, which covered up most of his scar. Then they headed to the White Castle fast-food joint. It was a place Phat couldn't seem to resist getting a bite to eat in, whenever in the Windy City.

While Phat was inside the restaurant along with his boys, Ace decided to remain outside in the Navigator and made a call to Paris via FaceTime.

"S'up, bae?" Ace asked once Paris appeared on the screen of his iPhone.

Paris smiled. "Hey, my love."

"Is everything good with you?"

"Well, I have to work overtime tonight, and since you're not in town, I don't know who else I can have pick up Adonis and watch him." She sighed.

"How 'bout you just have Mika do it. And don't trip, I'll be back home tomorrow."

"Ace, I don't know what the hell you're supposed to be doing, but it better not be anything that's gonna get you in any trouble."

"Told you, I'm takin' care of some business."

"That's all it better be."

"And I did get tatted. See." Ace pulled his shirt up enough for her to see the ink. "Plus, I did some shoppin', and I picked up you and Adonis some things you'll like."

"What is it?" Paris asked with excitement.

Ace grinned. "You'll see whenever I make it home."

"Just make sure you bring your ass home to me and your son soon."

"Bae, just give me until tomorrow night. I should be home by then."

"Alright."

"What you mean to me?" Ace cared to know.

"Everything," Paris cooed.

"Nothin' less. Hug my son for me."

Ace ended the call with Paris once noticing Phat along with the others exiting the restaurant. Once they all loaded back into the Navigator, they headed back to the hotel for the remainder of the night.

The following day, Phat was on the phone with his plug, Legs, putting things into place. Once he ended the call, he then instructed Nice to help him recount the paper, and Ace and Troy to load up the pistols. Though Phat made the trip routinely to meet with his plug, he always wanted to be sure that everything went accordingly. Once it was time to go and meet with the plug, they loaded into the Navigator with the re-up money and strapped up.

They rolled through Inglewood, which was located on the south side of the city. In order to even enter the area, being that Legs was well-connected with the Gangsters throughout the land, the plug had given Phat a G-pass. Phat was to meet with Legs at Murray Park, which had been dubbed Murder Park by the locals, due to its reputation for countless gangland murders.

It was afternoon when they arrived at the park, and for the most part the park was scarce. They pulled into its parking lot and parked beside the plug's matte black Panamera Porsche. Legs set near the hoops on the bleachers, surrounded by some of his gang members. Phat stepped out the Navigator hauling the tote bag containing the cash and the others followed. As they approached Legs, his gang members eyed them closely. Phat sat beside the plug while Ace and Nice and Troy stood there on security.

"Do I gotta count the cash, or are you sure it's all there?" Legs said once Phat handed over the bag to him.

"I'm sure. Count it if you want," Phat suggested.

Legs handed over a backpack to Phat which contained the work. "If the cash isn't all there, then you'll know how far my reach is." Phat knew that was a subliminal threat.

"I haven't ever came short, and I ain't gonna start now. As long as the work right, there isn't any reason for me to shortchange you."

"Good thing we still have that understandin'." Legs smirked.

Phat and the others started towards the Navigator, when a few of Legs's gang members blocked their path. Before allowing them to draw their guns, Ace quickly drew the MAC .11 from his waistband, then Nice and Troy followed suit. They were all patient but ready to dump. Neither Legs nor his gang members seemed to be at all troubled. Legs gestured for the Gangsters to let Phat n'em pass.

Once Phat n'em loaded into the Navigator, they perpetually observed their surroundings for cops and robbers as they moved through traffic. Getting on highway I-95, they were on their way returning to the Mil, where there were sure to be cops and robbers lurkin'.

•••

After putting on a sensational performance on stage, Savvy came strutting her stuff through the club, making her floor rounds. She rocked red lace lingerie and red leather thigh-high stilettos. Ace didn't mind that she danced on a pole, it don't make her a hoe. After all, once the club closed at three in the morning she was leaving home with him. So he encouraged her to go get the bag.

Ace was seated at a more secluded table alone nursing a glass of Henny. Whenever he showed up at the club he normally kept a low profile.

Several of the niggas in attendance who lusted over Savvy stopped her as she walked through the club, and Ace realized they were willing to cash her out. One of the niggas in particular, who was dripped in ice, gently grabbed Savvy's hand and worked his mouthpiece on her. Ace was quite sure the nigga was spitting some of his slickest lines at Savvy. After gesturing for him to give her a second, Savvy strutted away with the nigga admiring her ass. Ace was sure that Savvy was aware of the effect of her allure on niggas.

"So, did you enjoy the show?" Savvy asked as she stepped up and found a seat on Ace's lap.

"Fa sho! You did your thang, boo," Ace commended her.

"I know, right." Of course she knew.

"Noticed homeboy all over you."

"You mean Toucan. He wants a lap-dance, that's all."

"Haven't seen him in here before. Is he a regular?"

"He comes in here mainly to check in on his girls."

"And I suppose this Toucan nigga would like for you to be one of his girls also," Ace followed up.

Savvy smacked her lips. "This ain't that, nigga. And Toucan knows that much by now."

The nigga Toucan was one of the city's pimps, although he didn't wear no suits or ties, because he was considered a tennis-shoe-pimp. Toucan had a stable of hoes working the stroll and some working the pole. He was brown-skinned with a bald-fade and gold teeth, and he had the gift of gab.

Ace took a swig of his drink. He noticed Toucan cut his eyes at his table and said, "You better go before your boyfriend gets the wrong idea."

"Seems like he already has," Savvy quipped, referring to Ace. She grabbed his drink and downed its remains before rising from Ace's lap and then returning to Toucan's table.

Ace knew Savvy was a bad bitch that niggas would thirst over. And he figured he could use her allure as leverage in one way or another.

•••

Pulling up in front of Neesha's crib, Ace parked the Acura. He was there for a dropoff / pickup being that she'd called him for a re-up. Ace had been fronting Neesha pounds of loud and she was moving them with ease, and they both were making good money. Ace's only problem with Neesha was that she had too many people in their business because she talked way too fuckin' much. Although, being that it was known she was selling for him, Ace figured no one would be willing to rob Neesha knowing the aftermath. Thus far, their business was booming.

Ace grabbed the pound he brought with him from out of his stash, which was behind the driver's door panel, then stepped outta the car and headed up to Neesha's front door. He rapped on the door and a moment later, it was pulled open by Star. The two gave one another a onceover before their eyes met, the mutual attraction was undeniable. Without exchanging a word, Star stepped aside and Ace stepped inside the house.

"Bitch, who's at my door?" Neesha asked Star as she entered the front room. Then she noticed it was Ace. "Oh, hey Ace. Thought you might've been my baby daddy. His ass get on my damn nerves. Anyway, what's up?"

"Here's yours, now where's mine?" Ace said as he pulled out the pound and handed it to Neesha.

"Lemme go and grab you yours. I'll be right back." Neesha headed for her bedroom.

Star was seated on the couch while Ace stood. He noticed she had Stone's name tatted over her left breast. Only problem Ace had with Star choosing to be with Stone was that he felt she went against the rule and fucked with an opp. Ace knew he and she weren't ever together but he still didn't feel it was cool. And Stone knew she used to be with Ace.

"Do you love Stone?" Ace wanted to know, breaking the silence.

"Why, Ace?" Star shifted in her seat uncomfortably.

"Even if you do, you and me know what it is."

Star folded her arms and crossed her legs. "And what is it?"

"It's mine." Ace smirked and Star didn't even object.

Neesha returned with the payout from the last front and handed it over to Ace and he began counting it. "It's all there, Ace. You know I ain't gonna play you like that," she assured.

"And I ain't gonna let you play me, Neesha," Ace told her as he continued to count.

"Anyway. You know that nigga Skinny been going around the hood claiming you sold him some bad dope. He even told me that shit when he came by to buy some weed."

Ace gave her his undivided attention. "So I heard. Listen, next time Skinny bring his ass by, make sure you call me."

After Ace had sold Skinny the eight-ball, Skinny claimed it was baking soda residue. And then Skinny decided to spread claims around the hood that Ace's whip-game wasn't proper, and if niggas wanted straight drop, they should shop with Stone instead. Ace figured Stone had a part in the sabotage, and Ace had to nip it in the bud immediately because it was bad for business.

After making sure the money was all there, Ace headed outta Neesha's crib. He came upon Quincy who was making his way up the porch steps. Quincy stepped aside and allowed Ace by him without a word, and Ace didn't even pay the scary-ass nigga no mind. He stepped down to Mika's crib and entered the front door, finding his sister in the kitchen cooking.

"Hey bro. Where you coming from?" Mika asked as she stirred the pot of mac & cheese on the stove top.

"Neesha crib."

"That bitch talks too damn much for me. You know she told me that you got her selling weed for you now. And I'm sure I ain't the only one she's told." She shook her damn head. "Anyway. Paris told me about your problems. I thought you wanted to do right by her. I get tired of her crying to me about your ass."

"Sis, don't worry about Paris. I got her," Ace replied.

"If you say so." Mika seemed unconvinced. She switched topics. "I'm surprised Gee not with you. He acts like he's too damn grown to listen to me anymore."

"Lil bro just growin' up, that's all."

"Well, I'ma kick his grown-ass outta my house if he keeps running the streets and shit." Mika looked to Ace with serious eyes. "Ace, do your all to look after baby bro in them streets," she told him.

"I'm my brother's keeper," Ace swore.

Afterward leaving Mika's place, Ace was headed for his car when he noticed Reverend Johnson pulling open the passenger door of the Cadillac for his wife to step out. Ace acknowledged the Rev with a nod of the head and in turn, Reverend Johnson told Ace to have some decency and pull up his pants, which Ace obliged. As Ace went to step into his car, Star emerged from Neesha's crib carrying her and

Stone's toddler daughter on her hip. The two held each other's eyes before Ace entered his Acura and then pulled off.

Around the corner, Ace parked in front of the trap spot. Glen, Poppa, and Bookie all approached the car and hopped in. Glen took up the passenger seat and the other two occupied the backseat. Ace rolled up a blunt and they passed it around, all getting high off the Kush Ace had copped from Abdul. Lately, he'd been copping pounds of weed from Abdul for the low.

"Who the fuck is that nigga?" Ace wanted to know as he observed an unfamiliar packboys trappin' on his corner. Being that the packboy didn't belong to his crew, pushing packs on Ace's turf was prohibited.

"That's a nigga from around the way named JJ. Heard he's down with Stone's crew now," Glen said.

Ace hit the blunt.

"Go and let him know that Stone's crew don't got no G-pass over here."

"Say no more," Poppa responded and then hopped out.

"We'll let the nigga know what it is," Bookie added as he followed suit.

Ace and Glen remained in the car while they watched Poppa and Bookie step to JJ. Poppa pulled his pole and stuffed it to JJ's ribcage and then Bookie began stripping JJ of his pack and cash, and he even snatched JJ's Cartier frames off his face. Afterwards, Bookie warned JJ to never come back around again, and as JJ began to hurry away Poppa kicked him in the ass.

Ace and Glen stepped outta the car with Poppa and Bookie who were laughing at JJ's expense. For a lil while they posted in front of the trap, taking turns servin' smokers. They all agreed they were hungry, and Glen volunteered to go and grab them something to eat from Popeye's. As Glen set off on his way to grab them a bite to eat, Ace headed inside the trap while Poppa and Bookie remained posted outside trappin'.

While Ace set on the couch watching *Boyz n the Hood*, his iPhone rang. He answered and it was a collect call from Cain. It had been several weeks since Cain last called and Ace had been anticipating him calling. He accepted the call.

"Say it ain't so, Ace," Cain breathed.

"What're you tryna say?" Ace asked, thrown.

"Nigga, I'm sayin' Tia told me how you tried to shoot your shot at her while she was in the club, and then you tried to take her home and fuck her. Thought we was better than that!" Cain's tone was aggressive.

Ace sat straight up. "You got it twisted. It was Tia who actually tried to shoot at me, until I checked her ass. Been waitin' on you to call, so I could let you know she ain't no good for you."

"Ace, my girl ain't gonna lie to me about nothin'. So nigga, miss me with that shit!" Cain barked.

"Cain, you gonna charge me up over that bitch, when all I done is keep shit one-hunnit with you. Bitches like Tia get niggas smoked. And when you touchdown, then nigga, I advise you to leave that bitch alone and get your mind right. Maybe if you stop thinkin' with your dick then you won't end up with your dick in the dirt," Ace asserted.

Cain took a brief moment before calmly replying, "Don't get caught lackin'." He hung up the call in Ace's face.

Apparently, Cain had allowed Tia to manipulate him into believing Ace had come on to her, when in fact she'd come on to Ace. The hoe knew Ace would expose her so she had twisted the story to make it seem as though Ace was the

one who was disloyal to Cain. And now Cain felt some type
of way towards Ace.

These hoes ain't loyal, Ace mused and shook his head.

His thoughts were cut when the door flew open and
Poppa and Bookie hurried into the trap supporting the weight
of a badly beaten Glen. His left eye was swollen shut and
upper lip was busted with blood leaking. Ace jumped up and
hurried over to Glen, he was heated seeing his lil brother
beat up badly.

"Fuck happened, Gee?" Ace wanted to know heatedly.

"JJ n'em jumped me at Popeye's. The nigga JJ took my
Glock and pistol-whipped me with my own shit. I'ma smoke
JJ bitch-ass!" Glen managed to say through his swollen lips.

Ace told the trio, "Grab some sticks. Let's go and spin
on them niggas."

The gang rode in Ace's Acura all strapped as 22Gz's
"Careers" played in the background. Knowing where JJ hung
out on the regular, Ace n'em was lurkin' for the nigga.
Glen's eyes darted in search of JJ, and he had murder in his
eyes. Bookie spotted JJ with some of his crew all posted up
in front of the corner store. Poppa was eager to jump out and
air out the opps. But Ace told them to be easy, and then he
pulled down the dark back alley with the headlights out.

Once Ace pulled over, he remained in the car while Glen,
Poppa and Bookie hopped out with guns in hand. The trio
crept through a gangway towards the front street where JJ
and his crew were posted and oblivious to the imminent
threat on their lives. Glen didn't hesitate to pop out the
gangway bustin' and neither did Poppa and Bookie.

Ace heard the countless shots being let off. While he
awaited Glen, Poppa, and Bookie to return to the car, he
peeped a nigga come staggering through the gangway
clutching his side from a bullet he took. Ace left the car

idling as he jumped out, gripping his FN and insidiously approached the opp who'd collapsed onto the ground. It was JJ.

"RIP," Ace hissed while standing over JJ with the FN leveled on his chest, then pulled the trigger.

Boc, boc, boc!

Ace made his way towards the car after he murdered JJ. Glen, Poppa and Bookie came hurrying through the gangway for the car as well. Once they were all inside the Acura, they skirted down the alley leaving behind a fuckin' murder victim.

Chapter 15

Ace was kickin' it with Adonis for the day. Although being in the streets consumed lots of his time, Ace also cared to spend time with his son. He just wanted to make a better way for Adonis, because Ace didn't want his son growing up and getting involved in the street life like himself. Ace wanted more for his son, even though he himself seemed content with gettin' it out the streets.

Ace had brought Adonis along for a haircut. After they had gotten cut up Ace, paid the barber and then he and his son bounced. While they rolled through traffic Ace allowed Adonis to sit on his lap and pretend to drive. Normally, Ace rolled with his pole across his lap, but he kept it beneath the seat whenever his son was rolling with him.

"You hungry, lil homie?" Ace asked.

"Yeah." Adonis nodded his head.

"What you wanna eat?"

"Mommy always get me a Happy Meal."

"Then I'ma go and get you a Happy Meal too."

Ace made a stop at the nearest McDonald's, where he walked in to place their order. Once they were back in traffic, as Ace drove, Adonis sat in the passenger seat and wasted most of his French fries around the car and barely even ate his burger. More than anything, Ace knew that Adonis just wanted the toy which came along with the Happy Meal.

Ace's next stop was to the car dealership. Now that he had a nice amount of G's stacked up, he was looking to cop himself a more modern and luxurious car. With summer in approach he wanted a whip that he could glaze in. Ace, along with his son, browsed around the dealership and checked out the various different brands and models of vehicles. Though the vehicles were pre-owned they were as good as new.

There was a 2016 red Infiniti G35 that Ace took interest in. It wasn't long before a clean cut, suit and tie wearing car salesman approached Ace, offering him a welcoming smile and his hand for a shake and introduced himself as Carl.

"Nice ride," Carl said. "Has touchscreen control, push starter, automatic gear, peanut butter leather seats, the works. And there's not many miles on it," He opened the driver's door for Ace to get a closer look at the interior and Adonis climbed inside behind the steering wheel pretending to drive. "Apparently your son likes the car very much. But how much do you like it?"

"This much." Ace pulled out a bankroll from the pocket of his Balmain jeans, counted out the sixteen thousand, eight-hundred-and-fifty-dollar price listed on the vehicle and cashed out. He and Carl went into the office, where Ace signed an ownership document and the title to the vehicle.

"She's all yours." Carl smirked and tossed him the keys to the Infiniti.

Ace left the Infiniti at the car dealership with plans to return for it the following day. Thirty minutes later, he and Adonis cruised down Capital Street on the way towards the hood.

"Why we can't ride in your new car, Daddy?" Adonis said.

"Because I gotta come back for it," Ace told him. During the ride, Adonis kept turning up the volume loudly on the stereo and Ace turned it down. "Your ass better not do it again." But Adonis did it once more and Ace popped him on the hand, then Adonis got the point and sat back in the passenger seat.

Arriving in the hood Ace parked in front of the trap spot, where he took his son along with him inside the trap. While Ace was in the front room bagging up some work that he was to serve a nigga, Adonis ran around playing with Glen. Glen roughed up Adonis, who tried to run over to his dad, and Ace nudged him back over towards Glen wanting him to learn to fight back.

"Stop actin' like a crybaby," Glen taunted Adonis.

"Shut up, bitch!" Adonis cursed him.

Ace's iPhone chimed and he peeped it was a text-message from Paris. She texted him that she was outside. Ace didn't like whenever she just showed up in the hood unannounced. He stuffed his FN on his waist and made his way outside then approached Paris's Accord.

"Paris, what I tell your ass about comin' around here without lettin' me know," Ace said.

"Thought you might want me to pick up Adonis after I got off work," Paris responded.

"You already know I'ont like you bein' in the hood."

"And Ace, I don't like our son being in the hood neither."

"Don't bring your ass around here again without lettin' me know first. A'ight?" Ace checked her.

"Alright, Ace. Now would you please go and bring me Adonis."

Ace went and grabbed Adonis and then brought him out to Paris. Once he put Adonis into his car seat then Paris went on her way. Returning back inside the trap, Ace took a seat on the couch beside Glen, who had Beast-Mode lying across his lap.

"What's on your mind, big bro?" Glen asked, noticing that Ace seemed bothered.

"It's Paris. Apparently, her ass don't like it whenever Adonis is in the hood with me. Like I won't protect him with my life," Ace griped.

"Paris knows you won't let shit happen to him without puttin' your life on the line. But she's just doin' what any good mother would to protect her baby. Wish our moms had been half as good of a mom to us as Paris is to your son."

Ace looked over at his brother. "Moms might've made us, so we're her babies. But she didn't do shit for us, the trenches raised us," he said, his tone flat.

"I know. And Mika wants us to just let Moms back into our lives." Glen scoffed. He may have resented their mother even more than Ace, being that he hardly knew her.

"Don't get me wrong, Gee, I care about our moms. I'm still her baby, but I'm a savage in these streets," Ace stated. He stood and started placing the work from the coffee table into a backpack. "Look, I got serves to make so I'ma get with you later."

Stepping out the trap spot, Ace was headed towards his Acura parked near the curb. He had the pole on his waist and carried the backpack containing a quarter-key of yae on his way to make a serve. Looking up and down the dimly lit block, it seemed quiet enough on this night. Once Ace stepped up to his whip, as he went for the driver's door, he then peeped the unmarked Magnum crawling down the street towards him and knew it was the dirty cops, Lucas and Bradshaw.

Shit, Ace cursed introspectively, understanding that if he was caught with the gun and drugs in his possession, then not only would the dirty cops shake him down, but he'd go back to prison. However, he refused to allow either.

Once Ace took off on foot, Lucas jumped out the Magnum and gave him chase. Darting towards a gangway, Ace disregarded Lucas's order to freeze. As he hit the gangway, Ace pulled his FN and sent shots at Lucas who ducked out the way, then drew his service weapon from its holster and returned shots.

Boc, boc!

156

Blam, blam, blam!

Ace heard bullets zip by him as he continued fleeing through the gangway, and then he jumped the gate and was scot-free. He was sure that Lucas knew exactly who'd shot at him, and now Ace knew that Lucas would have it out for him personally. Ace realized that if Lucas got the chance then he'd riddle him with bullets and justify it as self-defense, so Ace was willing to hold court in the streets.

Ace called up Savvy to come scoop him up from the hood because he knew it wasn't smart for him to go back to the trap.

•••

Two weeks had slid by since Ace's shootout with Lucas, and Ace hadn't been in the hood much to avoid a run in with the dirty cop. But still Ace didn't neglect the hood.

As Ace was pushing the Acura towards the hood's liquor store his iPhone rang and he peeped down at the cell in the cupholder and saw the call was from Neesha. He answered.

"You told me to call you when Skinny come by, and he's here right now," Neesha said, talking quietly.

"Anybody with him?" Ace wanted to know.

"Um, yeah. It's like two people outside in his car parked in the front."

"A'ight. I'm on my way. Just unlock the back door for me."

"I got you."

Ace headed to Neesha's crib, he took notice of the car Neesha mentioned parked in front of her place, but Ace couldn't see exactly who was inside past its tinted windows, more than likely there were a couple of his boys with straps.

Pulling into the alley Ace parked, jumped out the car, and then made his way for the back door of Neesha's house. Before making his way inside, Ace pulled the FN from his waistband. Once inside, Ace made his way towards the front room where he could hear Neesha talking with Skinny. Little did Skinny know, Neesha had set his ass up.

When Ace stepped into the front room, as soon as Skinny noticed him there Skinny jumped from the couch onto his feet. He peered suspiciously at Ace then to the gun Ace held leveled on his chest. Ace stepped up on Skinny and patted him down and confiscated his pistol, stuffing it in his waistband. He didn't need for Skinny to try anything that would cause him to have to off Skinny in front of Neesha, because Ace knew he'd have to also off Neesha to keep her from talking too fuckin' much.

"This how you gonna do me, Neesha,?" Skinny said, feeling deceived. "You a connivin'-ass bitch!"

"Nigga, she don't got shit to do with this. Now step out-back so I can talk to you," Ace told him assertively. He pressed the muzzle to Skinny's back and shoved him out the back door. Ace forced Skinny back up against the house and pointed the FN in his face.

"Fuck is this shit about, Ace?" Skinny feigned ignorance.

"Heard about you claimin' I sold you some bogus yae and tellin' niggas to shop with Stone instead of me. I'ma tell your ass this shit once if I hear about you doin' some shit I'ont like again, then I ain't gon' have a problem with smokin' you whenever I catch you. Now keep my name out your damn mouth," Ace stated coldly.

Once Ace cut Skinny loose then Skinny hurried away towards the front street. He heard the car that was awaiting Skinny skirt off. Part of Ace wanted to body the nigga right then and there because he knew Skinny could come gunning for him. Yet Ace wasn't worried because he was savage with his.

Making his way back to the Acura, Ace dipped around the corner and came upon Glen posted out on the block with Poppa and Bookie. They were servin' smokers.

"Where you comin' from?" Glen asked as he stepped up to the car.

"Neesha crib. She had called me over to deal with the nigga Skinny," Ace said.

"And how'd it go?" Bookie wanted to know.

"Took the bitch-nigga pole and then told him to keep my name outta his fuckin' mouth, or else." He handed over the gun to Glen.

"Shoulda smoked his ass, 'cause you know that nigga gon' run to Stone," Poppa input.

Ace scoffed. "Stone can get it too. Look, I'ma get with you niggas later."

Ace pulled off on his way to Savvy's place. He'd been staying by her place a lot more frequently, being that the two were getting closer. Plus, his stash was there. Arriving at Savvy's place, Ace noticed her car wasn't there. Using the key she'd given him, Ace let himself in the house and came upon Dre seated on the couch in the front room.

"Why you here while Sav gone?" Ace questioned.

"'Cause this my sis crib, that's why," Dre retorted and stood. "Besides, I was just leavin'. Let Sav know I stopped by." He shouldered Ace on his way out the front door.

That nigga lucky he's Savvy's brother, Ace contemplated.

There something about Dre that Ace didn't trust. He went and checked his stash finding it looked untouched. Afterwards he kicked off his Air Jordan's and then turned on the flat screen in the front room where he took a seat on the couch. He smoked a blunt while watching a Milwaukee Bucks basketball game. Getting the munchies, Ace went and grabbed some cold leftover pizza from the fridge because Savvy wasn't the type of bitch who cooked. While he ate the pizza and continued to watch the game, his iPhone rang. Ace answered, seeing that it was a call from Chedda.

"I'm steppin' out tonight, you rollin' with me?" Chedda asked.

"I'll pass. I'm chillin' with my side bitch for the night," Ace told him. Since Savvy didn't have to work the club tonight, Ace wanted to chill at the crib with her.

"Don't tell me your ass about to lay up with some side bitch, while you have Paris at home."

"Somethin' like that," Ace replied.

Chedda scoffed. "Ace, don't let some side bitch break up your happy home."

"Let me worry about my home with Paris. A'ight, Chedda?"

"Yeah, a'ight." Chedda knew Ace was going to do as he please regardless. He switched subjects. "Anyway. We'll be goin' to see Shane in a couple days, so have your paper set."

"Say no more."

"I'll be in touch." The two ended their call.

Having the bubble guts courtesy of the leftover pizza, Ace went into the bathroom to take a shit. Afterwards, he decided to freshen up and take himself a shower. He then dressed himself in a tank top and Nike sweatpants bottoms. When Ace returned to the front room, he noticed Savvy's Chrysler now parked out front through the window. He peeped her standing outside of a chameleon painted Cadillac CTS sittin' on rims, talking with the driver who turned out to be Toucan. Once Savvy turned and strutted away the 'Lac idled a moment while Toucan admired her phat ass.

160

Nigga, you can look but don't touch, Ace thought as Toucan drove away.

Ace held the door open for Savvy and as she stepped into the crib, she pecked Ace on the lips. She carried with her some shopping bags from a few outlets.

"Where your ass been?" Ace probed.

"Out shopping with Nina," Savvy answered. "I dropped her off on my way here." She put away the bags in the front closet.

"Tell your lil bro not to have his ass here when you're gone."

"I got you."

"And fuck was that nigga Toucan doin' trailin' you? You fuckin' with him or somethin'?" Ace pressed.

Savvy scrunched up her face and replied, "Uh-uh, Toucan isn't even my type. He seen me in traffic and pulled up on me. He just always tryna shoot his shot whenever he sees me," Savvy told him. She kicked off her UGGs and then took a seat on the couch.

"Best tell his ass to fall back."

"Ace, your ass is trippin' and shit right now. It's not even like that, so just let it go."

"Let me find out, Sav," he warranted.

Savvy stood and remarked, "You got some nerves coming at me like that when I ain't even your wifey." She steamed into the bedroom.

Ace knew Savvy had a point. He had Paris, who he was in love with, although he had love for Savvy. Making his way into the bedroom behind Savvy, Ace stepped up on her and grabbed her at the waist and pulled her close to him.

"My bad, Sav. A nigga just got love for your ass, that's all," Ace apologized.

"And I got love for you too, Ace. You're my nigga, and that's just how I want it to be."

Ace kissed her lips and Savvy slid her tongue into his mouth. He turned her around and bent her over the bed, then pulled down her fitted jeans, exposing her round ass. Kneeling behind her, Ace spread her cheeks and licked his tongue over her asshole causing Savvy to moan softly. Ace slipped his tongue from her rosebud to her pearl and Savvy arched her back, loving the feel of him pleasing her orally.

"Oooh... It feels so damn good, Ace!" Savvy cried out. She tooted her ass up, allowing Ace to slip his tongue deep into her asshole while he finger-fucked her pussy. "Hit this pussy from the back." Ace stood to his full height and pulled his sweats down, freeing his hard dick and then dug deep into Savvy's slit from behind.

"Shit, this pussy wet, boo," Ace groaned. As he stroked her, he dipped his thumb into her asshole and Savvy got off on the double penetration. She tossed her head back and took the dick as she came. Then Ace removed his dick from her pussy and slid it in her asshole. He enjoyed how she looked back over her shoulder at him making fuck faces. She reached back and grasped her cheeks, spreading them.

"Aahh... Shit, baby, I'm cummin' out the ass..." Savvy buried her face into the mattress and muffled her moans. Her asshole tightened around Ace's dick as he slid back and forth in her ass. He gripped her cheeks and slammed her ass back on his dick. Some strokes later, he bust a nut inside her ass.

Ace fell forward on her, panting. "That shit was bomb, boo. Now roll up a blunt and let's watch Netflix and chill."

•••

"On our next re-up, I wanna ante up the weight. With all of our trap houses, we can move more weight than we're currently movin'," Chedda was saying. He pushed the Audi through traffic while Ace rode shotgun.

"As long as it'll bring us in more money, then I'm with it," Ace agreed.

They were on the way to meet with Shane for a re-up. It had been already arranged that they would cop two-and-a-half bricks, plus Shane would front them that exact amount, therefore Ace and Chedda would be picking up five bricks in total. And they'd be dropping off the re-up money for this new load, plus the front money from the last load, which added up to a hundred and seventy-five grand. Ace and Chedda continued getting their money and weight up in the game.

"And once we put enough money together to open our own strip joint, then I won't be dealin' drugs as much because I'm tryna flip the game," Chedda added.

"I feel you."

"Speakin' of the strip joint, we need to make sure that ours have bitches that are as bad as your side bitch, Savvy. 'Cause shorty bad!"

"I know how we can make sure of that. I'll holla at Savvy because she'll be able to assist us in recruiting some bad bitches. Plus, I plan on havin' her work at our club," Ace told him.

Chedda glanced over at him and said, "You sure it's a good idea to mix pleasure with business?"

"Fam, I can handle my business."

"Enough said." Chedda dipped around a vehicle.

Arriving at Shane's auto detailing shop, Chedda pulled the Audi inside the spacious garage. The shop was a legitimate business, which Shane often used as a drug lair and drug distribution hub. Also, lots of drug-traffickers used the shop to have trap compartments installed inside their vehicles. Shane more so used the shop as a front in order to keep the feds off his ass.

Some vehicles were being attended to by mechanics while Shane and some of his crew lounged around. Chedda departed the Audi carrying a backpack and Ace followed. Shane stepped up and greeted them.

"C'mon, let's talk in private," Shane said as he led them to his BMW truck which was also parked inside the garage. He stepped into the passenger seat while his main man filled the driver's seat, and Ace and Chedda took up the back seat. Shane looked at them through the rearview mirror and asked, "Is that all the cash?"

"Not a penny short," Chedda replied. As he went to hand over the backpack, Ace halted him.

"Cash on delivery. Nothin' personal," Ace declared.

Shane smirked. "I understand, just business. Beneath the seat."

Ace reached beneath the seat and came up with a tote bag. He looked inside, finding the bricks. Chedda then handed the bag to Shane, who didn't even bother to look inside of it.

"I been thinking. After this load, I want to give you the entire next one on a front. This way we both stand to make lots of money," Shane suggested.

"How much product? Chedda asked.

"And what's the payout?" Ace wanted to know.

"Seven keys at two hundred forty-five G's. How does that sound?" Shane observed both men reactions through the rearview mirror.

"Sounds like a deal," Chedda spoke up.

Ace piped in. "Just make sure it's pure cocaine."

"Done," Shane assured.

After wrapping shit up with Shane, Chedda and Ace were on the expressway heading back towards their trap spot. Ace watched every move in case the feds were on them and Chedda had to drive real smooth with those bricks on them. Icewear Vezzo's "100K" played in the background at a lowered volume.

Chedda switched lanes, heading for the exit ramp. "With those seven bricks Shane's gonna front us, we have a chance to get rich."

"But with competition like Stone, there's no doubt that he wants to take us out, so we gotta stay savage," Ace warned him.

"Maybe it's time we get Stone out the way."

"I was thinkin' the same."

"Then we'll send some hitters at him."

Ace looked over at him and stated, "I'ma hit Stone personally."

"It's been a long time comin'." Chedda smirked.

Chedda knew Ace had been wanting to smoke Stone for the longest. And now seemed to be the right time. With Stone out the way, he'd be one less opposition they would have to worry about getting in the way of them eating. But they knew it was other niggas hungry for more so eventually, they would have to tend to other opps.

Martell "Troublesome" Bolden

Chapter 16

Ace and Paris lay in bed after putting Adonis to sleep. They were watching *Queen & Slim* on the flat screen TV. Lately, Ace hadn't been spending a lot of his nights at home, being that he was either sleeping in the trap or staying nights with Savvy. Of course, Ace loved having a life with Paris and being a family with her and his son. He just had a lot of other shit going on in his life.

Paris snuggled back against Ace, liking the feel of her body pressed against his. It was nice to have him home for a night because she was growing tired of spending nights without him. Part of her was beginning to believe he had a side bitch who he spent his nights with when he wasn't home. But then again she figured Ace was just in the streets all damn day and night. Paris just wanted for Ace to be there for her and Adonis.

"Ace, I can't stand those nights when you're not here. I dealt with that while you were in prison and I shouldn't have to now," Paris told him.

"I hear you, Paris. And if I could then I'd be here with you every night. But you know some nights I get wrapped up in the streets," Ace replied.

Paris turned, facing him. "You sure it's not some other bitch, Ace?"

"Paris, don't even ask me no shit like that. You know a nigga love your ass," Ace responded coolly. Part of him felt wrong for cheating on Paris, but he believed what she didn't know wouldn't hurt her.

"And I love you too. Which is why I worry when you're in them streets," she stressed.

"You don't have to be worried, 'cause when I'm in them streets I can take care of myself. But I ain't gon' brag about what I do for the streets. All that matters is I'm here now."

Ace began passionately kissing Paris. He palmed her ass and pulled her close. The two helped one another out of their wears. Paris then climbed atop him and straddled his lap. She planted kisses on his neck. Grabbing his hard dick Paris guided it into her wet pussy. He sat up sucking her titties as she gyrated her hips feeling him deep within her.

"Mmm... oh, yesss... I love it," Paris moaned. She tossed her head back and then began bucking harder on the dick and it hit her spot. Ace continued flicking his tongue over her rock-hard nipples and sucked them into his warm mouth, massaging each nipple with his full lips. Paris liked the feel of her nipples in his mouth while his dick was in her pussy at the same time. She pushed him back on the bed and kissed him greedily while bouncing on his hardness.

"Damn, bae... oooh, shit... You ridin' the fuck outta a nigga dick," Ace grunted as Paris repetitively slid her wet-shot up and down on his big dick. He palmed her ass and assisted her with pouncing on him. Paris planted her petite hands on his chest and dug her manicure into his flesh out of pleasure as her pussy came. Feeling her cum, Ace rolled her onto her back and then mounted her, he pushed her legs back exposing her wet slit and slid his piece inside her walls.

"Just like that, Ace... Oooh, my goodness... Fuck this pussy, nigga!" Paris cried out in pleasure. The dick dug deep in her snug love tunnel, she could feel it in her stomach! She tried running from the dick but Ace held her steady as he drilled in her pussy.

"Take it, Paris. Take this dick, boo," Ace asserted, causing Paris to become wetter with his dominance. He lowered one of her legs and held the other up over his shoulder as he rapidly thrust his dick inside her wetness. Paris moaned out his name repeatedly which encouraged him to fuck her deeper. "Oh, shit!" he grunted as he busted a nut.

Ace rolled beside Paris in bed, both were satisfied with their quickie. Paris wrapped herself within Ace's arms and he spooned her. It was moments like this that Paris wanted with Ace, but he always seemed to let his street life get in the way of his love life. Although she knew it didn't mean he didn't love her. Ace was also just in love with the streets.

Ace's iPhone rang, interrupting the moment. He rolled over and grabbed the phone off the nightstand and noticed the call was from Mika. *Hell is sis callin' me so late for?* he wondered. Ace answered.

"S'up, sis? Everything good with you?" Ace said concerned.

"Ace, where are you right now?" Mika asked frantically.

"I'm at the crib. What is it?"

"It's Neesha. Something happened to her. It's all on the news right now."

Ace sat up in bed and used the remote to turn the TV to Fox6 news. It was breaking news, with the newscaster standing before Neesha's place, which was sealed off with yellow tape. There were cops and squad cars littering the street.

"Fuck happened?" Ace wanted to know.

"She was shot to death during a robbery. I heard the gunshots and when I looked out the window, I saw a tall, skinny dude running away with bags in his hand. Ace, Neesha didn't deserve that," Mika stressed.

"Mika, if Twelve come askin' you any questions, make sure you tell them that you didn't see shit, you didn't hear shit, and you don't know shit. Just leave it in the streets," he told her before they ended the call.

Ace couldn't believe what had happened to Neesha. He was more upset about her being killed than he was about her being robbed. Partly, he felt at fault for her murder because had he not had her selling loud for him, then she wouldn't have been involved in a game so deadly. He didn't know exactly who murdered Neesha but he had an idea of who it could be. And if Ace found out who the suspect was, then he'd be sure to make him a victim of homicide.

•••

Sitting in the rental car, Ace and Glen watched a trap spot from down the street. They were on the lookout for Skinny. After hearing around the hood that Skinny was the one who murked Neesha, Ace's suspicion was confirmed and he had been looking for the nigga. No one could identify Skinny as Neesha's killer, although Ace was sure he was. He figured it was Skinny's way to get back at Neesha for setting him up for Ace. And Skinny robbing her in the midst of it made Ace feel like Skinny was tryin' him.

Ace had heard that Skinny was using this particular trap as a weed house. He was anxious to catch this nigga and put a hole in him. The block was only dimly lit by the streetlights and rain misted on this spring night.

"Ace, you sure this the right spot?" Glen asked. He sat in the driver's seat.

"Yeah. At least it's the spot I was told," Ace replied. He was closely observing the spot.

"Let's just run up in there and off the nigga."

Ace looked over at his lil brother. "Gee, you just drive. I'ma off this nigga myself."

"Say no more. But why do you want the nigga Skinny so bad for yourself?" Glen wanted to know.

"'Cause I feel it's my fault he smoked Neesha. Not to mention, I told Skinny I'll murk his ass if he do anything else I'ont like. Listen, Mika has been afraid for you since what happened to Neesha on my account."

Glen snorted. "Well, she don't have to be, 'cause I ain't afraid to ride or die."

"Don't you get it? That's what Mika is afraid of, Gee. And she made me vow to look after you in these streets. And I will, even if I have to go out bustin'."

"Ace I'll go out bustin' for you too."

"No doubt. But, Gee—" Ace was interrupted when he peeped the nigga Skinny emerge from the spot. He then gripped the Draco in his lap and stated, "This nigga mine."

As Skinny lit up a Newport cigarette, he made his way down the porch steps, heading for his car parked curbside. He didn't notice the car with tinted windows parked down the street with Ace lurkin' in it. He had heard Ace was looking for him, so he stayed strapped for any beef. On the other end, Ace slipped out the car with his Draco in hand. He slunk down the block trying to go unnoticed. As Skinny reached for the handle of the car door he peeped Ace creeping, he then pulled his Glock from his waist and he and Ace matched guns.

Boc, boc, boc, boc, boc!

Boom, boom, boom!

Both niggas ducked out of the line of fire as bullets zipped by them, only inches away. With each squeeze of their triggers, flames from the muzzles lit up the dim block. Ace took cover behind a tree while Skinny ducked beside his car. Through exchanging shots, chunks were knocked from the tree and windows were shattered on the car, although both niggas avoided being shot.

Skinny shot back over his shoulder as he fled towards the spot and Ace chased after him, letting off a barrage of gunfire. Once Skinny made it inside the spot as he tried closing the door, bullets from Ace's Draco tore through the timber door striking Skinny twice in the stomach and once in the ribcage piercing his lung and caused him to collapse. Ace barged inside the spot and leveled the Draco down on Skinny.

"Nigga, told you I will body your ass if you pull anymore shit," Ace growled.

"G-go to... hell!" Skinny managed to remark as he chased his breath.

"I'll meet you there."

Boc, boc!

After dumping two slugs in Skinny's dome and murdering him, Ace hurried back to the rental car and then Glen skirted off down the street. Now that he had murked Skinny, Ace felt vindicated although he knew it still wouldn't bring back Neesha. Ace and Glen just rode in silence, because they understood the concept of silence and secrecy.

Chapter 17

The club was lit and seemed to be filled to capacity. There were some rich niggas and several bad bitches in the building. Lots of cash was being tossed and plenty of bottles were flowing. Not to mention, there was a stripper on the main-stage poppin' her pussy on a handstand. Ace and Phat were in attendance, just chillin' and poppin' bottles. They were seated at a secluded table near the back where they could observe the scene.

Phat sipped from his bottle of Ace of Spade. "I wanna offer you an official spot in my crew. I can use a nigga like you as my underboss."

"All due respect, Phat, I'm my own boss. But we can do business together," Ace told him.

Phat smirked. "I can respect that. Then we'll keep it strictly business, nothin' personal."

"Sounds good." Ace sipped at his glass of Henny. "Speakin' of business, me and Chedda plan to open our own strip joint. You know, somethin' legit to keep the feds off our backs. Maybe you should think about goin' legit yourself after what happened to Baller, since you're one the lucky ones who ducked that indictment."

Phat shifted in his seat. "Look, Baller got too sloppy, that's why he got indicted. And I didn't get lucky, instead I was smart enough to cut off Baller when the feds did their sweep. A'ight?" Ace detected that Phat seemed defensive.

"I guess cuttin' off Baller was in your best interest," Ace responded dubiously.

Nina came strutting through the club, rockin' a silver leather bikini top and boy-shorts with a pair of pumps. She stepped up to Ace and Phat's table.

"Hey, Ace. Who's your homie, with his fine ass?" Nina said as she checked out Phat, who was iced out.

"Phat," he spoke up on his own behalf.

"And I'm Nina." She smirked. Nina looked to Ace and told him, "Savvy wanna see you in a private room. I'll keep your homie Phat here company for you." She took a seat on Phat's lap.

After drowning the remains from his glass of Henny, Ace made his way towards the private room. When he stepped inside the room he found Savvy lying across on the black suede couch, wearing nothing but a teal lingerie set and her red-bottoms. Without a word Savvy used her index finger to coax him over to her, and Ace took a seat on the couch. Savvy began kissing him as she pulled his dick out from his Rock Revival jeans and stroked it to hardness. She then straddled his lap and slid her wetness down on his dick and a light moan escaped from her lips. Ace planted his hands on Savvy's small waist while she bucked up and down on his dick.

Ace thought the pussy was so fuckin' good. He slipped her nipple into his mouth and gently sucked and tugged on it with his full lips. He slid his hands down to Savvy's ass then began slamming her down on his hardness. As the dick hit her spot, Savvy tossed her head back, entranced by the feeling of his large dick deep within her wet pussy. Her pussy grew wetter as she came.

Savvy was so turned on and she wanted to pleasure Ace so bad, so she dropped onto her knees and took his big dick into her mouth. Ace bit down on his lower lip while he locked eyes with Savvy and she greedily sucked his piece. He palmed her skull and guided her mouth up and down on his dick until he busted a nut, and Savvy swallowed his semen and licked the dick clean.

"Damn girl, you did that shit," Ace said as he zipped up his jeans. "I better be the only nigga you give this type of attention to in the club."

Savvy stepped into her thong. "Trust, if it's not you then another nigga don't stand a chance," she assured.

"Good. Anyway, I noticed that nigga Toucan in here tonight."

"And, what about him?" She slid on her brassiere.

"And I wanna talk to you about the nigga." Ace pulled her onto his lap. "So, me and Chedda plan to open up our own strip joint. The thing is, we want some of the baddest bitches to work there. So, I'll need you to persuade Toucan to have some of his girls to work at our club," he expounded.

"And what makes you think he'll be persuaded by me?"

"Sav, we both know the nigga likes you. Just use that to your advantage."

"Alright, I'll holla at him. But I can't guarantee you anything," Savvy told him. "Now lemme go and get ready to take the stage."

Returning to the table, Ace came upon Phat, who was still accompanied by Nina. He could tell the two had hit it off. Waving over a waitress, Ace ordered himself another glass of Henny. Nina decided to go see Savvy now that Ace had returned.

"Apparently, y'all got a vibe," Ace commented, seeing that Phat kept his eyes on Nina.

"Yeah, I like the vibe she givin' me," Phat responded.

"Just know that Nina is a cool bitch, although she ain't shit but a sack-chaser."

Phat took a swig from his bottle. "Good thing I got my sack right."

Ace peeped the nigga Toucan checking one of his girls. He was sure that once Savvy talked with the nigga about the proposal to have more of his girls work in his and Chedda's club, then Toucan would see it as an opportunity to make more money. Although Ace didn't like the idea of Toucan being in charge of the girls that would be working in the club, he knew Toucan would provide some bad bitches. Ace would just use Toucan to get ahead of the game.

The DJ announced Savvy and she took to the stage and put on a sensational performance as niggas made it rain on her.

•••

Riding through traffic, Chedda was on his way to make the serve while Ace rolled along. They were in Chedda's Audi with Moneybagg Yo's "Time Today" playing in the background. Over time, Chedda had managed to really get his weight and money up a lot in the game. He was up three birds and three-hundred-some G's. Now he was living good off the game, a nice crib, a few whips, and business ventures. And Ace was still tryna get his own money and weight up just as much. Although the two never let money come between them.

Pulling into the parking lot of Taco Bell, Chedda parked beside a light gray Range Rover. The nigga Rex stepped out the Range looking around perpetually and then entered the backseat of the Audi. Ace thought the nigga seemed to be acting paranoid and he gripped the pole in his lap, just in case. Rex was a stocky nigga with a bald head and gold teeth, who was known for getting money throughout the streets, and he had his block on lock. Not to mention, the nigga had a squad of shooters on deck. Chedda had been servin' Rex for a few months and their business was always good. Rex had called for a half-brick this time around, which was more than he'd normally cop.

After Chedda made the drug transaction with Rex, they parted ways.

"That nigga was actin' 'noid to me," Ace mentioned.

"I'm sure it's just he's used to meetin' with me alone," Chedda replied. He pulled the whip outta the parking lot into traffic. "So, I been checkin' into shit concernin' the strip joint. And I took a look at a couple of potential spots. Bein' that we're goin' into business together, I wanna give you a chance to take a look at the spots yourself."

"Fam, I trust you to handle business the right way," Ace told him. He didn't care to have much to do with handling the business, he just wanted to have a share in it. For the most part, Ace handled business in the streets.

"Enough said," Chedda replied. He glanced over at his boy and said, "Notice you been dealin' with Phat a lot lately."

"Just tryna get my money up, that's all. The nigga did offer me a spot in his crew."

"And?"

"And I turned it down. Told Phat I'm my own boss and he respects it," Ace expounded.

Chedda braked at a stoplight on 27th Street. "Ever since Baller got jammed up, Phat has been tryna run the game," he remarked.

Ace shifted towards him. "What you sayin', Chedda?"

"I'm sayin' sooner or later, Phat gon' have to be taken out the game if we gon' run it."

"The game is cold but it is fair," Ace declared. He understood that once he turned down Phat's offer to join his crew, then he was considered a threat, being that Phat knew Ace was out to get rich the savage way.

They were on their way towards the hood. As they passed a dry cleaner, Ace noticed Marco emerge from the establishment. He hadn't been able to catch Marco for a couple months after the nigga ran off with the work Ace fronted him. Marco was talking into his iPhone as he stepped to the trunk of his Lexus IS sittin' on twenty-four-inch chrome Forgiato rims in order to place his dry cleaning inside. It was still daylight out so Ace wouldn't just murk him on the spot, although he wouldn't let the nigga get away.

"There goes the nigga Marco bitch-ass, pull up on him," Ace said and gripped the pole in his lap.

"Say no more." Chedda pulled up right beside the Lexus.

Ace jumped out the Audi with his FN in hand and advanced on Marco then pressed the muzzle to his head. "Don't try me," he forewarned as he patted the nigga down, finding no pole.

"Dawg, what the fuck!" Marco said frantically and dropped his phone. He couldn't believe he was caught lackin'.

"Shut the fuck up and get your bitch-ass in the trunk!" Ace demanded as he whacked Marco over the head with the pistol once. And without putting up a fight, Marco climbed into the trunk then Ace took his keys before slamming the trunk shut. Ace hopped inside the Lexus and pulled off with Chedda trailing.

They arrived at Mitch's garage. Ace had paid Mitch in dope to store the Lexus there and had the mechanic strip it of its rims which were replaced with spare tires. The car would remain there until he was done with Marco. Once Ace opened the trunk, Marco had fear in his eyes while Ace stood over him with the FN pointed at Marco.

"Thought you could just run off with my shit and get away with it Marco?" Ace growled.

"Ace, I-I was gonna p-pay you. I s-swear," Marco cried. Ace pressed the muzzle to his forehead. "Nigga, I want what you owe me. Now tell me where the stash at."

"How I know if I tell you where's the stash at then you won't kill me?"

Boc!

Ace popped Marco in the chest. "You don't know," he threatened.

"A'ight, a'ight! I-I'll tell y-you!" Marco caved, nursing his weeping bullet wound. "It's at my apartment on 25th and K-Kilbourn Street. You'll f-find the shit in the bathroom beneath the s-sink stashed in boxes of detergent." He was chasing his breath. "A-Ace, you can take it all, p-please just don't h-harm my bitch and kids."

"If you tellin' the truth, then I won't."

Ace drove the Lex to Marco's apartment with Marco still inside the trunk bleeding to death. Ace had Chedda trail him there. In front of the apartment complex, Ace parked, stepped outta the car with his Milwaukee Brewers cap pulled down low on his head, and the FN on his waist and started towards Marco's apartment. Being that it was now night out, Ace was disguised by the dark. He approached the door and drew his pole and knocked. A moment later, a chick holding a newborn opened the door a crack, and once she noticed the gun in Ace's hand she attempted to quickly slam shut the door. But Ace spotted a foot on the door preventing the chick from shutting it, he then forced his way inside and the chick shrieked.

"Bitch, shut the fuck up," Ace demanded, grabbing the chick by the nape of her neck. "Take me to the bathroom."

As the chick led Ace into the bathroom he noticed the second child, which was a toddler, seated in the bathtub taking a bath. Ace made the chick sit on the edge of the tub with her kids close by.

"Mama, who is he?" the toddler asked curiously.

"Shhh," the chick shushed the toddler.

Searching beneath the sink, just like Marco had assured, Ace found the two boxes of laundry detergent, one containing cash, the other yae. He warned the chick not to leave the bathroom until he was gone then he hurried out the apartment. As Ace came out, Chedda pulled up the Audi from down the street. Once Ace hopped inside the car then Chedda skirted off. Marco was left there in the trunk of his own Lexus for dead.

"That nigga Marco had me fucked up for thinkin' he was just gonna take my shit like that. Only thing a nigga takin' from me is a bullet," Ace ranted.

"Fa sho," Chedda concurred.

"You know how we do it, we'll split everything."

"Keep it. Besides, I ain't the one who Marco took it from."

"Say no more."

Ace had been dropped off by Chedda at Savvy's place. When Ace entered he came upon Savvy's homegirl, Nina, who was seated on the couch in the front room.

"Hey Ace. You coming to the club tonight? I know you gonna bring along your baller homeboy," Nina said hopefully.

"Maybe some other time. And I'll be sure to bring Phat with me," Ace responded on his way towards the bedroom with the boxes tucked underneath his arm.

In the bedroom Savvy was prepping to go to work at the club for the night when Ace stepped in. He removed his FN from the waistband of his Gucci denim jeans and then set it along with the boxes on the nightstand before sitting on edge of the bed. Savvy knew Ace was watching her as she went into the closet and pulled out a few lingerie sets and pairs of heels for work and then she placed the items in inside her Prada weekend bag.

"Damn, what you lookin' at?" Savvy asked bashfully.

"You. Bring your bad ass here," Ace told her suavely. She ambled over to him and he pulled her on top of him then began planting kisses on her neck while gripping her ass.

"Boy, would you stop. Nina out there waiting on me."

"Let her wait." He kissed her lips.

Savvy pulled herself from his arms and stood between his legs. "Your ass know I gotta get to work while you tryna start something. Nigga, didn't you get enough last night and this morning?" She smiled.

"You know a nigga can't seem to get enough of you." He sat up and held her at the waist.

"Well, not right now, player," Savvy told him. She heard Nina call for her and replied, "Just gimme a sec, girl." Then she turned back to Ace.

"When me and Chedda open our own club, then you won't have to run off on me."

"I know, right. Anyway, what's in those boxes?"

Ace grabbed the boxes and dumped out the bundles of G's and Ziplocs of ounces on the bed. "A nigga just tryna get his money and weight up, that's all." He smirked.

"I see," Savvy replied.

"Why don't you go ahead to the club. I'll catch later."

Savvy grabbed up the Prada bag and her keys and said, "Later." After pecking him on the lips, she made her way out the house with Nina.

Ace counted up the money and dope he'd taken. He then put it all away in the closet inside the hidden compartment with the rest of his stash. Altogether, in just the six months

Ace had been off lockdown, he'd managed to come up on some over a brick of yae and a hundred and thirteen grand in cash. While tryna get rich and living the savage life, Ace was piling up money, drugs, and murders.

Chapter 18

There was a block party taking place in the hood that was put together by Reverend Johnson. With all of the bad going on in the hood, Rev thought it would be best to see everyone have a good time. The residents were playing games and listening to music and barbecuing. Ace and Chedda even had their BMs Paris and Antoinette there with the kids. Star and Red were also present. And outta respect, Ace and Chedda had their crew keep the crack-heads off the block for the day. For once in a long time, they just wanted to have a good day.

Ace and Chedda were sitting on the front porch steps of the crib that used to be Neesha's. The hood was still mourning the loss of Neesha, there was a shrine of teddy bears and balloons set out in front of the house. Some even wore T-shirts with a picture of Neesha's face on it. Reverend Johnson had done the sermon during Neesha's funeral.

Ace just had to off Skinny for taking her life, and he didn't regret it. And even though it was an unsolved murder, most everyone in the hood had an idea that Ace was responsible for murdering Skinny, including Reverend Johnson.

"One of these days I'ma move out the hood," Chedda said.

"Just don't forget where you came from," Ace replied.

"And what about you?"

Ace peered at his boy and said, "I'd stay in the hood forever if every day was like this one."

"Well, the day isn't over just yet," Chedda let him know.

Reverend Johnson stepped up carrying two plates of food, one in each hand. "Thought you two would want some of this good ol' BBQ." He smiled and handed over the plates to Ace and Chedda, who thanked him. "No, young brothers, thank the Lord."

"Rev, the block party is a good turnout," Ace said.

"Been a while since this block was so peaceful," Chedda added.

"And I couldn't have done it without you all making sure there are no sins disrupting the neighborhood for the day at least. Listen, I don't agree with your lifestyle but only God can judge. Believe it or not, I wasn't always what one would call a saint. So I understand that every sinner have a future just like every saint have a past. Always remember that. I better go and tend to the grill." Rev headed away.

While Ace and Chedda sat on the porch downing the BBQ, Ace looked over to Paris, who was talking with Mika and Antoinette. All of their kids were running around together playing tag. Paris caught his eyes and she playfully stuck out her tongue at him. He did love her a lot, even though he was fuckin' off on her. But she and his son meant a lot to him. He peeped Star checking him out while she and Red and Kiki talked among each other. One thing for sure, Ace didn't want to cause any drama on the block. Ace and Chedda stepped over to Glen, Poppa, and Bookie who stood near the curb talking shit and passing around a blunt.

All was going well, up until Stone decided to show up and crash the party. He was there looking for Star.

"Bitch, didn't I tell your ass not to come to this shit?" Stone barked at Star and grabbed a fistful of her hair. "Grab my fuckin' daughter and get in the car."

Reverend Johnson stepped to Stone. "Young man, this isn't the time nor place for you to be acting like this. Why don't you let the girl and baby stay and have a good time? We're just trying to have church in these streets."

"No point in church, 'cause the preachers can't keep the poles from clappin'. These are my streets, " Stone retorted. Once he went to snatch up Star, then Rev pulled her behind him. Stone shoved the older man onto the ground. "Mind your own!"

Ace hurried over and pushed Stone. "Nigga, fuck is your problem?" He then helped Reverend Johnson to his feet.

"For starters, you're my problem." Stone stepped into Ace's personal space. "Think you run shit around here, like a nigga won't get at you. You'll need the Rev at your wake."

"I'm warnin' you to take Star and your baby and just go, Stone."

"Nigga, you got me fucked up!"

Stone took off on Ace, landing a blow square on his jaw. Ace countered with combo of punches to Stone's face. While they fought, Paris and Star cried out for their men to stop, both holding their babies. Chedda and the others made sure none of Stone's boys jump in while the two brawled in the street. Stone was getting the best of Ace, he busted Ace's nose and blacked his eye. Having had enough, Ace pulled the FN from his waist and aimed it in Stone's face, which showed no sign of fear. He didn't give a fuck about killing Stone front of his own son, in front of Stone's daughter, or no one else.

"Enough!" Reverend Johnson boomed. "This ain't the way either you young brothers want things to end. Not like this in front of these women and children. Over what, money, power, respect? Can't take any of it with you when you die."

Ace reluctantly put his pole away and growled, "Get the fuck on, Stone." He thought better against murkin' Stone right then and there.

"You gon' wish you woulda used that," Stone stated.

"That'll be your death wish," Ace remarked.

Stone headed for his car with Star in tow. Once they entered the car, Stone skirted off with malice aforethought.

Ace and Stone both knew that the body count in the hood was bound to rise until either of them were dead.

•••

A crowd of onlookers surrounded the two dogs as the K9s attacked one another with the intent to kill. The dog-fighting ring was taking place inside the garage behind Ace n'em trap. Glen fought Beast-Mode on the regular for wagers, and thus far, his dog proved to be a killer. And this time around, Beast-Mode was put up against a vicious pitbull.

Beast-Mode and the pitbull charged at one another with their sharp teeth exposed as they bit at the other's neck. The pitbull had some size on Beast-Mode, although Glen had trained Beast-Mode to be a certified killer. Beast-Mode managed to sink his teeth deep within the opposing pit's throat area, and the more the pit tried squirming free, Beast-Mode clamped down tearing its flesh. The pit gasped for air as Beast-Mode growled and violently shook up the helpless pitbull.

Ace stood off to the side with Chedda watching the dog-fight, along with Bookie and Poppa.

"Beast-Mode is about to kill that mutt," Ace said.

"He knows it's either kill or be killed," Chedda added. He puffed the blunt and looked to Ace. "Speakin' of, you know after that beef at the block party the other day, you gon' have to kill Stone before he kills you."

"I'ont sleep no beef, you know I'm on top of everything. That's why I put word out in the hood that Stone ain't to be fucked with, and any nigga who chooses to fuck with him will get the beef too."

"And once the nigga Stone is out the way, then not only won't we have to worry about beefin' with him over the hood, but we won't have continue to compete with him in the game."

"That's what you call killin' two birds with one Stone." Ace smirked.

The beef between Ace and Stone had the hood divided. Thus far, there were no shots exchanged between them although niggas on either side were bound to be smoked. So Ace knew to keep his strap on him at all times, and he was sure Stone would stay strapped also. The way Ace saw their beef, it was either he or Stone. And it was better Stone than him.

Counting a handful of cash from his winnings, Glen stepped up with a blood bathed Beast-Mode at his side. "That's a good boy." He patted the dog on its head and it wagged its tail. "Told you Beast-Mode is a killa!"

•••

In the hood, Ace pulled the Acura to the curb at the liquor store. He stuffed the FN on his waist before stepping out the whip and then entering the store. Upon entering, there was a nigga standing at the register, so Ace got in line behind him. As Ace awaited his turn at the register, he peeped two juvenile delinquents in the aisle stealing candy and Abdul was too busy ringing up the paying customer to notice. Ace couldn't help but smirk at the thought of doing it himself when he was around the juvenile's age.

Sometimes you gotta get it how you live, Ace mused.

Abdul said, "How can I be of help to you, Ace?"

"Let me get a box of Swisher Sweets blunts," Ace replied. He paid for the blunts and Abdul handed them to him. "I'll be in touch."

Ace departed the store. As he made his way towards his whip, someone flicked a cigarette butt out of the crack of the window of a silver sedan parked at the curb. He couldn't see who was inside the sedan, its windows were tinted and it was night out. Ace clutched the butt of his pole just in case, but then the sedan pulled off down the street. Maybe he was just too on edge due to all the beefs he had with niggas. There was death around the corner and he was down to shoot it out.

Stepping into his Acura, Ace pulled off down the street on his way to the block. Once he turned onto the block he pulled to the curb in front of Mika's house. He stuffed the FN on his waist then stepped out the whip. On his way towards the house, he waved at Reverend Johnson who sat on his porch and waved back. And as usual, the Rev told Ace to pull up his sagging jeans, which Ace obliged. Upon entering, there was Mika and Glen seated on the couch in the front room. He knew they were expecting him. Mika had called Ace earlier, saying that she wanted to talk with him and Glen but he didn't know about just what exactly.

"S'up sis, what is it you wanna talk to us about?" Ace inquired.

Mika patted the seat beside her and said, "You should sit."

"Sounds to me like whatever it is we're gonna need to smoke on it." Ace took a seat and began rolling up a blunt.

"I wanna talk with both of you about Mama," Mika told her brothers who sat on either side of her.

Glen scoffed. "Big sis, I'ont wanna hear shit about Moms because she ain't here for us."

"Well, too bad, because you're gonna hear it," Mika asserted. "I know Mom has been absent for most of our lives. But she still loves us. I went to visit her, and she told me she wants to see you two, because she don't want to see neither of you end up dead in the streets."

"I'ont wanna see her ass. And I ain't goin' to," Glen huffed.

"Gee, let's just hear sis out," Ace chimed in.

"Fuck that. She won't convince me to go see Mama. I ain't no lil boy anymore, so I'ont need Mama for shit."

"That's your problem Gee, you think you're too damn grown to listen anymore. All I try to do is tell you right. But if you won't listen to me, then I want you out of my house," Mika told him firmly.

Glen jumped to his feet. "Mika, if you want me out then I'll get out!" He hurried for the front door. Mika started to go after him, but Ace stopped her.

"Mika, I'ont wanna see Moms neither but maybe it's best to. Let me go talk to Gee alone," Ace said.

Making his way out the front door, Ace came upon Glen sitting on the porch steps. He took a seat beside Glen. Ace knew that Glen resented their mom maybe even more than he did, because Glen was born while she was in prison. So he understood why Glen never wanted to step a foot in a prison again. Although Ace felt it was probably best that Glen go and see her.

Ace handed Glen the rolled blunt. "This'll ease your mind."

"I need it." Glen lit up the blunt and took a heavy pull on it.

"Listen lil bro, I'ont wanna see that broad either but I think we both should. That way, we'll be able to tell her ass how we feel and hear her out. And I know the streets raised us, but always remember that Mika has been here for us. She been more like a mom than a big sister. So for that, we should love her," Ace expressed.

"You're right. I'll go and see Mom with you just so I can look her in the face. And as for big sis, I love her ass more than he knows."

"Then let's go back inside and let her know... Oh, shit!"

As Ace and Glen stood, the sound of a vehicle accelerating up the street caught their attention and there was a shooter hanging halfway out the window of the silver sedan gripping a .223 assault-rifle. As Ace and Glen went for their own guns, the shooter began airing them out.

Boc, boc, boc, boc, boc!

A fusillade of bullets flew at Ace and Glen, some leaving the house decorated with bullet holes. The two pulled their own guns and fired back at the sedan. The shooter braved the hail of bullets as he continued to let off the .223 with intent to kill. Glen popped the shooter in the arm, although the shooter never stopped bustin'. As the sedan sped away down the street, Ace leaped over the porch banister and chased behind the sedan with the FN airin' out the sedan until it made a sharp turn at the corner.

"It's gonna be okay, Gee!" Mika bawled. She had hurried outside once the shots stopped.

Turning back for the porch, Ace then found that Glen had been shot and Mika was on her knees holding his head in her arms. Reverend Johnson had witnessed the entire scene unfold from his porch, he prayed that Glen would survive.

Ace rushed onto the porch and saw that Glen was shot in the chest once. He then knelt beside Glen and tried applying pressure to the wound in his chest, but blood continued to pour through the crevices of his fingers. Glen's breaths grew faint, it seemed likely he would die.

"Shit, Gee, don't you dare die on me. Savages don't die!" Ace shouted, filled with frustration and panic, not knowing what else he could do to prevent the inevitable.

Watching blood flow from the gaping hole in Glen's chest while he tried to stop the bleeding took Ace back to the night he himself damn near died. He couldn't even imagine what was going through Glen's mind.

Ace could scarcely see the rise and fall of his brother's chest and, even as he watched, the blood began to seep slowly onto the porch instead of streaming thickly as before. Glen coughed up blood. No matter how badly Ace wanted to save him, he couldn't even if he tried his best. Then Glen took his final breath.

Peering into the tormented face of Mika, in close to a whisper, Ace uttered, "He's... he's dead."

"Nooo!" Mika broke down in tears. Her heart sunk in her chest like a stone through water.

Holding Glen's lifeless body in his arms, all Ace could think about is getting vengeance on whomever did this. Tears ran down his face, it felt like he was crying blood. With malice aforethought, Ace consciously vowed, *I won't be satisfied until whomever did this not breathin'.*

To Be Continued...
Rich $avage 2
Coming soon

Submission Guideline

Submit the first three chapters of your completed manuscript to ldpsubmissions@gmail.com, subject line: Your book's title. The manuscript must be in a .doc file and sent as an attachment. Document should be in Times New Roman, double spaced and in size 12 font. Also, provide your synopsis and full contact information. If sending multiple submissions, they must each be in a separate email.

Have a story but no way to send it electronically? You can still submit to LDP/Ca$h Presents. Send in the first three chapters, written or typed, of your completed manuscript to:

LDP: Submissions Dept
Po Box 944
Stockbridge, Ga 30281

DO NOT send original manuscript. Must be a duplicate.

Provide your synopsis and a cover letter containing your full contact information.

Thanks for considering LDP and Ca$h Presents.

Coming Soon from Lock Down Publications/Ca$h Presents

BOW DOWN TO MY GANGSTA

By **Ca$h**

TORN BETWEEN TWO

By **Coffee**

THE STREETS STAINED MY SOUL **II**

By **Marcellus Allen**

BLOOD OF A BOSS **VI**

SHADOWS OF THE GAME II

TRAP BASTARD II

By **Askari**

LOYAL TO THE GAME **IV**

By **T.J. & Jelissa**

IF LOVING YOU IS WRONG... **III**

By **Jelissa**

TRUE SAVAGE **VIII**

MIDNIGHT CARTEL IV

DOPE BOY MAGIC IV

CITY OF KINGZ III

By **Chris Green**

BLAST FOR ME **III**

A SAVAGE DOPEBOY III

CUTTHROAT MAFIA III

DUFFLE BAG CARTEL VI

HEARTLESS GOON VI

By **Ghost**

A HUSTLER'S DECEIT III

KILL ZONE **II**

BAE BELONGS TO ME III

A DOPE BOY'S QUEEN III

By **Aryanna**

COKE KINGS V

KING OF THE TRAP III

By **T.J. Edwards**

GORILLAZ IN THE BAY V

3X KRAZY III

De'Kari

THE STREETS ARE CALLING II

Duquie Wilson

KINGPIN KILLAZ IV

STREET KINGS III

PAID IN BLOOD III

CARTEL KILLAZ IV

DOPE GODS III

Hood Rich

SINS OF A HUSTLA II

ASAD

KINGZ OF THE GAME VI

Playa Ray

SLAUGHTER GANG IV

RUTHLESS HEART IV

By Willie Slaughter

FUK SHYT II

Rich $avage

By Blakk Diamond
TRAP QUEEN
RICH $AVAGE II
By Troublesome
YAYO V
GHOST MOB II
Stilloan Robinson
KINGPIN DREAMS III
By Paper Boi Rari
CREAM III
By Yolanda Moore
SON OF A DOPE FIEND III
HEAVEN GOT A GHETTO II
By Renta
FOREVER GANGSTA II
GLOCKS ON SATIN SHEETS III
By Adrian Dulan
LOYALTY AIN'T PROMISED III
By Keith Williams
THE PRICE YOU PAY FOR LOVE III
By Destiny Skai
I'M NOTHING WITHOUT HIS LOVE II
SINS OF A THUG II
By Monet Dragun
LIFE OF A SAVAGE IV
MURDA SEASON IV
GANGLAND CARTEL IV

CHI'RAQ GANGSTAS IV

KILLERS ON ELM STREET III

JACK BOYZ N DA BRONX II

A DOPEBOY'S DREAM II

By **Romell Tukes**

QUIET MONEY IV

EXTENDED CLIP III

THUG LIFE IV

By **Trai'Quan**

THE STREETS MADE ME III

By **Larry D. Wright**

IF YOU CROSS ME ONCE II

ANGEL III

By **Anthony Fields**

FRIEND OR FOE III

By **Mimi**

SAVAGE STORMS III

By **Meesha**

BLOOD ON THE MONEY III

By J-Blunt

THE STREETS WILL NEVER CLOSE II

By K'ajji

NIGHTMARES OF A HUSTLA III

By King Dream

IN THE ARM OF HIS BOSS

By Jamila

MONEY, MURDER & MEMORIES III

Rich $avage

Malik D. Rice
CONCRETE KILLAZ II
By Kingpen
HARD AND RUTHLESS II
By Von Wiley Hall
LEVELS TO THIS SHYT II
By Ah'Million
MOB TIES II
By SayNoMore
BODYMORE MURDERLAND II
By Delmont Player
THE LAST OF THE OGS II
Tranay Adams
FOR THE LOVE OF A BOSS II
By C. D. Blue

Available Now

RESTRAINING ORDER **I & II**
By **CA$H & Coffee**
LOVE KNOWS NO BOUNDARIES **I II & III**
By **Coffee**
RAISED AS A GOON I, II, III & IV
BRED BY THE SLUMS I, II, III
BLAST FOR ME I & II

Martell "Troublesome" Bolden

ROTTEN TO THE CORE I II III

A BRONX TALE I, II, III

DUFFLE BAG CARTEL I II III IV V

HEARTLESS GOON I II III IV V

A SAVAGE DOPEBOY I II

DRUG LORDS I II III

CUTTHROAT MAFIA I II

By **Ghost**

LAY IT DOWN **I & II**

LAST OF A DYING BREED I II

BLOOD STAINS OF A SHOTTA I & II III

By **Jamaica**

LOYAL TO THE GAME I II III

LIFE OF SIN I, II III

By **TJ & Jelissa**

BLOODY COMMAS I & II

SKI MASK CARTEL I II & III

KING OF NEW YORK I II,III IV V

RISE TO POWER I II III

COKE KINGS I II III IV

BORN HEARTLESS I II III IV

KING OF THE TRAP I II

By **T.J. Edwards**

IF LOVING HIM IS WRONG…I & II

LOVE ME EVEN WHEN IT HURTS I II III

By **Jelissa**

WHEN THE STREETS CLAP BACK I & II III

Rich $avage

THE HEART OF A SAVAGE I II III
By **Jibril Williams**
A DISTINGUISHED THUG STOLE MY HEART I II & III
LOVE SHOULDN'T HURT I II III IV
RENEGADE BOYS I II III IV
PAID IN KARMA I II III
SAVAGE STORMS I II
By **Meesha**
A GANGSTER'S CODE I &, II III
A GANGSTER'S SYN I II III
THE SAVAGE LIFE I II III
CHAINED TO THE STREETS I II III
BLOOD ON THE MONEY I II
By J-Blunt
PUSH IT TO THE LIMIT
By **Bre' Hayes**
BLOOD OF A BOSS **I, II, III, IV, V**
SHADOWS OF THE GAME
TRAP BASTARD
By **Askari**
THE STREETS BLEED MURDER **I, II & III**
THE HEART OF A GANGSTA I II& III
By **Jerry Jackson**
CUM FOR ME I II III IV V VI
An **LDP Erotica Collaboration**
BRIDE OF A HUSTLA **I II & II**
THE FETTI GIRLS **I, II& III**

199

Martell "Troublesome" Bolden

CORRUPTED BY A GANGSTA I, II III, IV

BLINDED BY HIS LOVE

THE PRICE YOU PAY FOR LOVE I II

DOPE GIRL MAGIC I II III

By **Destiny Skai**

WHEN A GOOD GIRL GOES BAD

By **Adrienne**

THE COST OF LOYALTY I II III

By Kweli

A GANGSTER'S REVENGE **I II III & IV**

THE BOSS MAN'S DAUGHTERS I II III IV V

A SAVAGE LOVE **I & II**

BAE BELONGS TO ME I II

A HUSTLER'S DECEIT I, II, III

WHAT BAD BITCHES DO I, II, III

SOUL OF A MONSTER I II III

KILL ZONE

A DOPE BOY'S QUEEN I II

By **Aryanna**

A KINGPIN'S AMBITON

A KINGPIN'S AMBITION **II**

I MURDER FOR THE DOUGH

By **Ambitious**

TRUE SAVAGE I II III IV V VI VII

DOPE BOY MAGIC I, II, III

MIDNIGHT CARTEL I II III

CITY OF KINGZ I II

Rich $avage

By **Chris Green**
A DOPEBOY'S PRAYER
By **Eddie "Wolf" Lee**
THE KING CARTEL **I, II & III**
By **Frank Gresham**
THESE NIGGAS AIN'T LOYAL **I, II & III**
By **Nikki Tee**
GANGSTA SHYT **I II &III**
By **CATO**
THE ULTIMATE BETRAYAL
By **Phoenix**
BOSS'N UP **I , II & III**
By **Royal Nicole**
I LOVE YOU TO DEATH
By Destiny J
I RIDE FOR MY HITTA
I STILL RIDE FOR MY HITTA
By **Misty Holt**
LOVE & CHASIN' PAPER
By **Qay Crockett**
TO DIE IN VAIN
SINS OF A HUSTLA
By **ASAD**
BROOKLYN HUSTLAZ
By **Boogsy Morina**
BROOKLYN ON LOCK I & II
By **Sonovia**

GANGSTA CITY

By **Teddy Duke**

A DRUG KING AND HIS DIAMOND I & II III

A DOPEMAN'S RICHES

HER MAN, MINE'S TOO I, II

CASH MONEY HO'S

THE WIFEY I USED TO BE I II

By Nicole Goosby

TRAPHOUSE KING **I II & III**

KINGPIN KILLAZ I II III

STREET KINGS I II

PAID IN BLOOD **I II**

CARTEL KILLAZ I II III

DOPE GODS I II

By **Hood Rich**

LIPSTICK KILLAH **I, II, III**

CRIME OF PASSION I II & III

FRIEND OR FOE I II

By **Mimi**

STEADY MOBBN' **I, II, III**

THE STREETS STAINED MY SOUL

By **Marcellus Allen**

WHO SHOT YA **I, II, III**

SON OF A DOPE FIEND I II

HEAVEN GOT A GHETTO

Renta

GORILLAZ IN THE BAY **I II III IV**

Rich $avage

TEARS OF A GANGSTA I II

3X KRAZY I II

DE'KARI

TRIGGADALE I II III

Elijah R. Freeman

GOD BLESS THE TRAPPERS I, II, III

THESE SCANDALOUS STREETS I, II, III

FEAR MY GANGSTA I, II, III IV, V

THESE STREETS DON'T LOVE NOBODY I, II

BURY ME A G I, II, III, IV, V

A GANGSTA'S EMPIRE I, II, III, IV

THE DOPEMAN'S BODYGAURD I II

THE REALEST KILLAZ I II III

THE LAST OF THE OGS

Tranay Adams

THE STREETS ARE CALLING

Duquie Wilson

MARRIED TO A BOSS... I II III

By Destiny Skai & Chris Green

KINGZ OF THE GAME I II III IV V

Playa Ray

SLAUGHTER GANG I II III

RUTHLESS HEART I II III

By Willie Slaughter

FUK SHYT

By Blakk Diamond

DON'T F#CK WITH MY HEART I II

Martell "Troublesome" Bolden

By Linnea
ADDICTED TO THE DRAMA I II III
IN THE ARM OF HIS BOSS II
By Jamila
YAYO I II III IV
A SHOOTER'S AMBITION I II
By S. Allen
TRAP GOD I II III
RICH $AVAGE
By Troublesome
FOREVER GANGSTA
GLOCKS ON SATIN SHEETS I II
By Adrian Dulan
TOE TAGZ I II III
LEVELS TO THIS SHYT
By Ah'Million
KINGPIN DREAMS I II
By Paper Boi Rari
CONFESSIONS OF A GANGSTA I II III
By Nicholas Lock
I'M NOTHING WITHOUT HIS LOVE
SINS OF A THUG
By Monet Dragun
CAUGHT UP IN THE LIFE I II III
By Robert Baptiste
NEW TO THE GAME I II III
MONEY, MURDER & MEMORIES I II

Rich $avage

By **Malik D. Rice**
LIFE OF A SAVAGE I II III
A GANGSTA'S QUR'AN I II III
MURDA SEASON I II III
GANGLAND CARTEL I II III
CHI'RAQ GANGSTAS I II III
KILLERS ON ELM STREET I II
JACK BOYZ N DA BRONX
A DOPEBOY'S DREAM
By **Romell Tukes**
LOYALTY AIN'T PROMISED I II
By Keith Williams
QUIET MONEY I II III
THUG LIFE I II III
EXTENDED CLIP I II
By **Trai'Quan**
THE STREETS MADE ME I II
By **Larry D. Wright**
THE ULTIMATE SACRIFICE I, II, III, IV, V, VI
KHADIFI
IF YOU CROSS ME ONCE
ANGEL I II
By **Anthony Fields**
THE LIFE OF A HOOD STAR
By Ca$h & Rashia Wilson
THE STREETS WILL NEVER CLOSE

By K'ajji

CREAM I II

By Yolanda Moore

NIGHTMARES OF A HUSTLA I II

By King Dream

CONCRETE KILLAZ

By Kingpen

HARD AND RUTHLESS

By Von Wiley Hall

GHOST MOB II

Stilloan Robinson

MOB TIES

By SayNoMore

BODYMORE MURDERLAND

By Delmont Player

FOR THE LOVE OF A BOSS

By C. D. Blue

Rich $avage

BOOKS BY LDP'S CEO, CA$H

Martell "Troublesome" Bolden

CPSIA information can be obtained
at www.ICGtesting.com
Printed in the USA
LVHW021532250721
693637LV00006B/119